BOOMERANG

After the birth of her first child Jo van der Walt, the young wife of a South African sheep farmer, discovers she is going deaf. Its effects on her life, in particular on her relationship with her husband Kobie, are serious. But when, through the help of Rob Stirling, an Australian doctor, a 'miracle' cure is achieved it comes back like a boomerang into the lives of Jo, Kobie and Rob. The stage is set for an explosive situation.

Joy Packer

Boomerang

METHUEN

First published 1972
by Eyre Methuen Ltd
Copyright © 1972 Joy Packer
Reprinted 1983 by
Methuen London Ltd
11 New Fetter Lane, London EC4P 4EE
Printed in Great Britain by
Butler & Tanner Ltd, Frome and London
ISBN 0 413 45010 4

AUTHOR'S NOTE

All the characters in this
novel are entirely fictitious

JOY PACKER
Cape Peninsula.
1972

CONTENTS

AUTHOR'S FOREWORD

The characters in this novel are fictitious.

So is the little market town of Verfontein, where English-speaking Jo was born, and the sheep farm, Springbok Spruit, belonging to Kobie's Afrikaans family, the Van der Walts. I have located the town and the farm somewhere between the Great and Little Karoo, east of the main railway running through the vast lonely Karoo plateau from Cape Town and the sea to Johannesburg and the highveld.

The word 'Karoo' is a derivation of the ancient Hottentot term 'Garob' which implied an arid, unfruitful, uninhabited area. This plateau includes over a hundred thousand square miles beyond the coastal belt of the Western Cape. Much of it is semi-desert covered with low bush and much is irrigated by boreholes, rivers and lakes (*vleis*) that may be in flood one year and dry for the next five! The climate, too is dry and famed for restoring damaged lungs to health – hot in summer and cold in winter with snow lying deep on the slopes of its many high mountain ranges, such as the Sneeuberg – not far from my fictitious Verfontein and Springbok Spruit.

The pastel colours and dramatic sunsets of the Karoo are the delight of artists and travellers, as is the blossoming of the plain after rain. It is the heart of South Africa's sheep country, and also contains fine racing stud farms. But the war against drought and the struggle to increase productivity is endless. There are many tenacious sheep-breeding families like my Van der Walts who have fought these battles for generations. Some have English roots, others are descended from the early 'trek-Boers', pastoral Dutch pioneers who grazed their flocks and cattle where they might as they trekked ever further inland. The indigenous dark-skinned people are as varied as the scenery, some pure Bantu, some coloured, often with the features and superstitions of the first little yellow Stone Age Bushmen or of the later Hottentots. All are South Africans.

More Afrikaans than English is spoken in the Karoo, and, where I have used Afrikaans words, I hope their meaning will be clear in their context.

The Jo and Kobie of my story are children of the Karoo. It chances to be their environment. But their cruelly difficult individual problem is universal. It *could* happen to any young couple anywhere.

PART ONE

Jo, Kobie and Rita

HOW COULD I HAVE DONE IT – I'M NOT NATURALLY
violent. Why? Above all, why? That's what they really want
to know.

'Did you intend to kill your husband?' the police have
asked me. 'Or were you trying to save your alleged lover?'

They've all hammered on at me since I've been in this
private ward attached to the European Women's Section of
Groote Schuur hospital. The police, the lawyers, the doctors,
the psychiatrist. Most of them are deadpan, asking their
questions for their various reasons, appearing to accept my
answers, neither condemning nor condoning, just trying to
get at the facts. After all, a trial for murder is pending. So
they need to know exactly what made me act the way I did
that night on the shores of the lake. So much hinges on that.
On *why* I did it.

All the same, Professor Rabinowitz, the senior gynaecologist here watches over me like a motherly dragon and when
he reckons I've been grilled long enough he intervenes with
his fine black eyes blazing and his caustic tongue lashing out,
putting even high-ranking police officers to flight.

He knows how important it is to me to keep this baby,
even if I have to lie in this room for weeks longer doing

exactly as I'm told. He understands that the baby, which has now quickened, holds the key to my future – if I have such a thing any more. When I first felt that flutter it was a message of hope as well as an announcement. I spread my hands over him – surely this is a son? – and whispered: 'Stick by me, little fellow!'

Dr Elizabeth Kidston was thrilled today when I told her I'd felt life. She too knows what it means to me. She's my psychiatrist. She's young for her job, thirty-two and has children of her own.

When she came this evening I'd already had my supper and the long shadows of the September dusk turned the mountain forests into a dark tapestry. I can see them from where I lie. The pines, and the oaks already in early leaf.

Perhaps because we're both young, or because she wants to establish a special bond between us, Dr Kidston likes us to use first names. I'm not Mrs Van der Walt to her, nor even Josephine. I'm Jo. And I call her Liz. I feel she's my friend, that she cares what becomes of me . . . She's tall and angular and wears her brown hair coiled in the nape of her long graceful neck; when she turns it the line of chin is pure and classic, but, oh, those wisps and strands that escape and mar the symmetry!

When I told her about the baby quickening – about being sure at last that he was still alive after all that ghastly nightmare at the lake and this past month's struggle not to lose him – her long bony face lit up and she leaned forward eagerly in the armchair by the window.

'How wonderful! I'm so glad for you. Now you've got the true incentive to live – '

'I'm young. There's so much to live for – and I've thrown it all away . . .' The familiar bewilderment overwhelmed me again. 'It was the all-time high success story – the miracle that got off to a flying start and came back like a boomerang to hit me straight over the heart.'

I buried my face in my hands.

She came to my bedside and pulled them gently away, forcing me to look into her penetrating eyes.

'Listen, Jo, you may have to stay in hospital for a while yet. We've been trying to help you – all of us here and your parents too, but now the time has come for you to help yourself. For the sake of this baby you're carrying —'

'How can I help myself? I don't know why I did it. We've talked it all through . . . then a shutter comes down . . .'

She drew the wooden stool from under the high hospital cot and sat on it, still holding my small hands in her strong ones.

'That shutter must be raised. I have a theory that you should try to be your own analyst. Write your story from A to Z, before and after . . . what you call . . . the boomerang miracle.' She relinquished my hands, but her eyes still held mine, detached and thoughtful. 'Miracles, you know, have odd side effects. That episode at the lake was one of them. Calamitous.' She hesitated.

'Go on,' I said.

'You're very articulate. Writing your personal story shouldn't be too difficult. Explore yourself and the cause. If you go at it quietly from the beginning you'll be able to face – and even explain – the end. Write from your own point of view of the things that happened to you – as *you* saw them and felt them. To hell with condemning yourself —'

'That may be done for me —' I cut in bitterly.

She didn't deny it, just stuck to her point.

'Go in search of yourself – and of the truth. Don't funk the truth. Will you try to do this? I'm positive it's the only therapy for you, Jo . . .' She was always so lucid and convincing.

She left me then with the dusk seeping into the room through a partly open window and the air beginning to grow chill. This was her way. To implant an idea and then vanish. No staying to argue. Just a bit hypnotic, perhaps.

Next day she brought me two foolscap-sized wirebound exercise books. I turned them over in my hands. On the cover was written STUDENT'S NOTEBOOK. STUDENTE AANTEKENINGBOEK. Oh, those Afrikaans omnibus words!

'Now make a start,' she said. 'Let's see what happens. I got you six ballpoint pens too.'

'Where on earth does one begin with this sort of nonsense?' I was half intrigued. A journey down the hard path of truth with your eyes wide open? It must of course lead to the lake and what happened there, but at least I might discover *why*.

She pushed the inevitable wisp of hair out of her eyes and grinned engagingly.

'Begin at the beginning – as far back as you remember.

That's point A. Let it be a record of events and emotions but try to hold on to the proper sequence. Don't become random. One thing leads to another, the cause to the effect.'

'Which came first – the hen or the egg?'

She laughed. 'I think you're on your way.'

All the same, the books lay beside my bed unopened, the pens untouched. The task was beyond me.

In the afternoon Mummy brought Gert to tea with me. It was his third birthday. She's taking care of him in the Muizenberg flat. She's very sweet with him.

Gert clambered on to the high bed and sat beside me swinging his sturdy legs.

'What have you got for me, Mom?'

He was all excitement, round blue eyes sparkling, crisp curly fair hair rising like a stiff little crest from his round crown. Mother had taken the precaution of smuggling my present for him into my room earlier in the week and I had it ready for him. He tore off the pretty gift wrapping with blunt, impatient fingers.

'A warship!' he cried. 'With guns. Boom-boom, bang-bang! All finish!'

My mother sighed. But I said:

'Good. It's a success. You chose the perfect toy, Mummy. Even at three it's natural to destroy . . . things . . . and people . . .'

I spoke toughly. A great rift had yawned between her and me since the episode at the lake. She couldn't forgive me for any part of it. I believe she held me wholly to blame. No

17

extenuating circumstances. Extenuating circumstances . . . oh, God!

'Gert!' I called suddenly. 'Come here!'

He ran to my bedside and quick as a monkey was up beside me.

'Feel here!' I put his little palms over my tummy to let him feel the new life quickening inside me. He knew about the baby, of course.

His eyes widened and his nostrils dilated as they often did in moments of emotion or astonishment.

'Like a flutterby,' he said. Then he wriggled away and back to his warship. He hadn't liked that 'flutterby'. It was a tiny voiceless threat to his own supremacy.

'*So*?' My mother was frowning. 'I think that was unnecessary, Jo.'

Her voice was cool and I knew at once that she was sorry my child had quickened. She would have preferred a miscarriage. She believed what Kobie had feared. Her tone roused my hostility. A great warm wave of protective love engulfed me. My womb should be a fortress for the child inside it.

My mother is a pretty woman considering she's over forty. Trim and precise with dark hair growing in a widow's peak off her broad brow. There are streaks of pewter in it. A neat nose, an oval chin. I'm supposed to be like her, but mine is a less controlled face, a more voluptuous mouth, more rebellious eyes. Mummy has been a teacher most of her adult life and her temper has been carefully curbed down the years. Only if you discipline yourself can you discipline others, she says. I've never been much good at disciplining myself or anybody else. Funny how you rebel against the virtues of those you most love and respect.

'How far back does memory go?' I asked her. 'Gert's three today. What will he remember of all this?' I made a vague gesture at the room flooded with primrose light.

'What you've just done could help to set it in his mind,' she reproached me. 'That gesture was physical and emotional combined. In the circumstances it would have been better never made.'

'Physical and emotional? I suppose you're right. I remember back to four. Very well indeed. My first real memory was one of resentment and anger. You should know.'

'You were an only child. Spoilt and with a high old temper.'

'So you and Daddy imported Kobie and Rita van der Walt into our house – to rub off the sharp edges.'

She rose. 'I'm going to ask nurse to make tea now and get out the birthday cake with its three candles.'

She knew how to scotch a conversation she didn't care about. But some strong breath of the past had blown upon the embers of recall and I felt the heat of a long forgotten rage burn up in me and obliterate nearly twenty years. There we were – the three of us – back in the little Karoo town of Verfontein on the day the Van der Walt children had first invaded our home. Rita and I were four, Kobie was five, and the memory of that day was branded into my deep consciousness – as no doubt it was branded into theirs; as quite possibly the 'flutterby' under his chubby palm would quiver uninvited from time to time in the nerves of my son, Gert.

'Begin at the beginning – as far back as you remember. That's point A.' Yes, Liz Kidston was right. And my mother – that clever teacher – was right too in realizing the strength of a physical and emotional impact combined. Suddenly I wanted to be done with the trappings of Gert's birthday. My fingers itched for the Student's Notebook and a ballpoint pen. Naturally the whole thing had begun – as it had ended – with the way Jakobus Gerrit van der Walt and I had felt about each other. And with his sister, Margerita, the golden child who grew to beauty and made the fourth in the final rectangle of our lives.

❄ 2 ❄

IT WAS BLAZING HOT AND DRY AS ONLY A MID-summer day in the Karoo can be. The stunted grey-green bush quivered with heat haze, the koppies and low flat-topped mountains stood ankle-deep in shimmering mirage. Everywhere, the thorn-bushes spread a drift of feathery yellow flowers pervading the brittle air of the veld with their soft sweet fragrance. The summer rains had fallen and the rivers were in spate. Drought was no stranger to our semi-desert, but that summer which brought Kobie van der Walt and his sister into my life was a year of plenty.

Although our little pastel market town of Verfontein baked in its shallow hollow it had the feel of an oasis, for the river bounded it and willows trailed abundant tresses on grassy banks. Birds and beasts reckoned the waterside was a nature reserve long before the town got around to agreeing with them and proclaiming the whole park area as a sanctuary. The long Main Street – wide enough to turn a span of sixteen oxen – was lined with splendid flame trees in scarlet blossom against the hot cobalt sky.

The Verfontein primary school was in Main Street near the market place and we lived on the other side of the school playground. Ours was an old colonial house, single-storeyed with a galvanized iron roof and a covered stoep on three sides. A long central passage led into the various rooms. The front room had a bay window which projected into a rose garden and commanded satisfying glimpses of Main Street through our cast-iron railing. A pergola loaded with green sultana grapes and red *hanepoots* sheltered a portion of our side stoep. So, of course, the birds came to share the fruit as it ripened. Their calls and twittering were the background music of my childhood, like the high shrilling of cicadas and the chirping of crickets.

My father, Joseph Carter, had expanded the old general store in the Square (once owned by his father) into the modern Zebra Supermarket and Shopping Centre. Daddy's great-grandmother had been a Jewess and that way-back infusion of Semitic blood into an English north country family had enriched its descendants with an exotic combination of business acumen and artistic appreciation. Daddy served his customers in the Zebra Supermarket and on Sundays he sang in the church choir, looking oddly miscast with his jet black hair and large oriental eyes. His grandparents had emigrated to South Africa in search of a wider future for their children who soon scattered according to their talents and their luck. Daddy, who loved the Karoo, settled in Verfontein to build on the solid business foundations laid by his father. With Zebra Supermarket he was on to a good thing.

Mummy, born and bred in the Cape Peninsula, had come to the Karoo because of a weak chest. She was a teacher in the English-speaking section of Verfontein primary school and she really loved her job. She got on well with the predominant Afrikaners, and the pure dry air cured her chest. Her teaching days finished when she married my father.

I was four when the Van der Walt invasion upset my apple-cart. My recollection seems crystal clear to me now, but then I've often been told about that fateful day, so memory has been well and factually supplemented. But the emotions are still capable of reviving and heating my blood.

That ordinary summer morning became sinister the moment I saw Lizzie, our coloured maid-of-all-work, and Livingstone, the Xhosa gardener, moving a second bed into my room – *my* room! I protested loud and clear.

'Your ma's orders, Miss Jo,' said Lizzie in Afrikaans. Her yellow wedge-shaped face with its high Hottentot cheek-bones was bright with amused malice. I fancy she'd had to put up with a good deal from me. An only child is not always lovable.

Livingstone spoke more soothingly in Xhosa.

'A nice little girl is coming to stay here and share your room. Her brother will come too and sleep in the spare-room.'

They chuckled when I stamped with rage, and Lizzie's Afrikaans aside to Livingstone was intended for my ears.

'Her ma said these kids would put our child's nose out of joint!'

Panic-stricken, I flew off to seek my mother and find out what monstrous nose-bashers were coming to assault me. To this day she knows I blame her for having let me learn about the advent of Kobie and Rita van der Walt the way I did. My intense resentment was spiced with terror.

I found her at her sewing-machine in the pleasant room that also served my father as a study. She swung round in dismay as I burst, panting and sobbing, into the room.

'Jo! Whatever's the matter?'

Frightened, threatened and angry, I was in no condition to express myself, but after a while she got to the bottom of my fears.

'Drat Lizzie! I told her to move that bed this afternoon. *Not* this morning.'

She drew me to her so that I leaned against her knee, still rigid with suspicion.

'Jo-Jo, it's true that Kobie and Rita van der Walt are coming to stay here with us. I'll explain in a minute; but first you must know that no one will so much as touch your little nose – except me, to give it a wipe, because it's running right now.'

She took her lavender-scented hanky and mopped at my tear-streaked face. She grew her own herbs in our garden and there were always little sachets of dried lavender among her handkerchiefs and undies.

'Nose out of joint indeed! That's just a silly expression. It means that a person used to being the one and only is going to have playmates —'

'I don't want playmates! I don't want another child in my room!'

Mummy ignored my passionate hostility. She hadn't been a teacher for years without acquiring the habit of authority.

'Listen to me! We live in a lonely district and our town has the only school for miles around. It's a good school but it doesn't take boarders. Kobie is nearly six and he must go to school *now*, this January term. Rita is four and a half, like you, and will go next year when you do. In the meantime I'll give her lessons in the mornings with you. Don't fidget, Jo, pay attention! This brother and sister are farm children. Their father has a fine sheep farm, but it's too far away for them to come to school every day. They have to stay in Verfontein. We have a big house and there is plenty of room for them. We must make them welcome here – as they will make you welcome at Springbok Spruit.'

She bulldozed my violent resistance.

'Another reason why Daddy and I want them here – and why their pa and ma want them to come to us – is because the Van der Walts speak more Afrikaans than English in their home and we speak more English in ours. Kobie and Rita will learn good English from us and you will learn good Afrikaans from them.'

'I learn Afrikaans from Lizzie —'

'That's kombuis Afrikaans – kitchen Afrikaans. Our country has two languages – English and Afrikaans. You must know them both properly.'

She wasn't talking like a mother any more. She had assumed her teacher's manner and achieved the shift that reduced me from pampered little daughter to ordinary pupil. All my life I've been conscious of this dual attitude. I was probably a highly emotional child and my father spoilt me, so when Mummy'd had enough of my temperamental displays she simply changed gear. The soft mother-look left her eyes, her lips tightened and she used a different, more metallic voice. The effect was to make me swallow my emotions. The turmoil remained but it settled in my tummy, a sickening hidden upheaval.

'When are they coming?' I muttered.

'This afternoon.'

When I heard the Van der Walt car draw up in Main Street outside our wrought-iron gate I fled into the garden and climbed the fig tree. Honey, my spaniel, followed me and sat under the tree. Like Honey, I was all ears. Voices, speaking in Afrikaans interspersed with English, floated out into the garden. The window of my room was open on to the section of the side stoep covered by the vine pergola.

'What a charming room!' That was Mrs Van der Walt who rolled the R of 'room' rather attractively. 'Don't you love it, Ritakie?' Another rolled R, and no comment from Ritakie. Only a loud sniff. So she was miserable too – this farm child.

'They're bound to be homesick at first. Don't let it worry you, Mrs Van der Walt. They'll adjust in no time. Children take so much for granted.' My mother, in her confident manner. This was a matter for mothers and there were no male voices.

'I know, and the sooner I get to my Agricultural Women's meeting and leave them to it, the better for all of us.' Mrs Van der Walt, very brisk.

'Ma! You can't go yet!' A small boy's tremulous entreaty in Afrikaans, a warm quick maternal response and the confused sounds that mean parting. Steps retreated along the passage, the front door closed and the garden gate clicked. The Van der Walt motor revved into life and receded down Main Street. Then the intruders and my mother were coming round the side stoep into the garden, and Mummy was saying in a penetrating tone for my benefit:

'I think Jo must be playing a game of hide-and-seek with you. See which of you can spot her first!'

I was playing no game that summer afternoon – and well my mother knew it. I was trying to escape from a detestable situation. That the wretched little Van der Walts might find it equally unbearable did not occur to me. Children are egoists.

Kobie and Rita, nervous and raw with parting, made no attempt to rush into our lovely wild garden at Mummy's suggestion. They hung back shyly, and there was a pause while I held my breath.

Suddenly the boy spoke in his high, clear, fluted voice, not quite sure of itself in English – or, perhaps, in these strange circumstances. But he was doing his best.

'I think I know where Jo is.'

'Well?' I could visualize my mother's raised dark eyebrows and her friendly smile. 'Well, Kobie?'

'There, in the fig tree.'

'I can't see her,' piped Rita, still sniffling a little.

'No,' said her brother in quick Afrikaans, 'but that is the tree the dog is guarding.'

'Well done! Go and talk to the dog. She's friendly. Her name is Honey.'

The girl stayed where she was with my mother, but the boy sprinted across the grass. He knelt on one knee and his blunt fingers caressed Honey's long silken ears. He whispered to her and she licked his face. They talked together for quite a time – Honey and Kobie. I listened and I looked down on them from the branch I straddled and for some strange reason my hostility began to evaporate. This boy loved my dog and my dog had made him welcome. His head was round, corn-coloured and curly and his shoulders were strong. He threw them back as he straightened up and stared into the wide leaves and grey branches of the fig tree. Suddenly he shouted triumphantly.

'Jo, I've found you!'

The next moment he was climbing the tree – *my* tree – and we met face to face, on my special bough. His tanned skin was mottled by the play of light and shade, his eyes were brilliant blue and, when he smiled, there were two big new teeth in the middle of his top gum. Just the place where I was missing a pair. It was funny, he looked as if he liked me. I know now that even then Kobie had a strong protective instinct. He's told me since that he knew quite well I wasn't playing hide-and-seek.

'You looked like a skinny little trapped creature right out on a limb, as far as you could go. Your hair was tangled and dark and your eyes huge and startled. Honestly, Jo, you looked like you might bite and scratch if I crawled one inch further towards you.'

Kobie's always loved wild things and I guess I was like a new small tree-animal to him that day. But I was also the daughter of the house and he'd been to the movies in Verfontein and knew how strangers address one another. So he gave me the human salute and said:

'Hi!'

'Hi!' I mumbled. And that was Round One to Kobie.

He looked round my tree and up and down it with interest. It was strong and complicated.

'This is a very good climbing tree. The best I've ever seen. I could make a tree-house up here.' It was an offhand suggestion. He recognized my territory and right of ownership, but he was offering to improve my property if I wished.

'A sort of nest?'

'Not a nest, 'n huisie – a little house.'

He began to describe it – how it could have a wall from here to there and a bit of a floor. No roof, because it was nice to look at the sky through green leaves . . .

'For me?' I asked, with restored confidence and the self-assurance of the only child.

He laughed. 'Sure. But you'd have visitors – me and my sister, people who like climbing.'

'Like Marmalade, our cat?'

'The cat'd make it a proper home. A house needs a cat. A dog can't climb, but Honey can stick around on the earth and be your special watch-dog.'

Even then Kobie could sweep resistance aside with his coaxing grin and his forceful charm. So he had his way. The tree-house was built.

🍂 3 🍂

FOR THE NEXT SIX YEARS WE THREE LIVED IN EACH other's pockets. During term time Kobie and Rita were our weekly boarders and most weekends I went with them to Springbok Spruit, the Van der Walt merino stud about a hundred kilometres from Verfontein.

Springbok Spruit, though I didn't appreciate it till several years later, was one of the most progressive properties in the Karoo. Mr Hendrik van der Walt held the traditional paternal viewpoint that the welfare of his black labour was his responsibility and Mrs Van der Walt actively supervised the organization of soup kitchens, school-feeding, crêches and a first aid unit. Many farmers thought his care for his *volkies* crazy, but others emulated the example of a farm which never had any difficulty in getting and keeping satisfied labour. Nor was any shooting allowed on Springbok Spruit, except occasionally a few springbok for the pot, when the wild herds of these lovely gay buck had to be thinned. It was a wild-life sanctuary.

When times were bad the surrounding farmers went to Mr Van der Walt for help and advice, as they had gone to his father and grandfather before him.

The farm – some ten thousand acres – was bounded by a

river which never ceased to be a thrill to us. Even in the dry season deep pools remained beneath their willows to remind us that the dusty water course would flow again in swirling majesty, and carry branches, dead sheep and other animals and reptiles with it. In flood it was frightening, covering the crops, rising to the treetops and bearing away the huts of the coloured and Bantu labour.

The farm was well watered with more than a score of good boreholes. It supported some three thousand merinos, a small herd of Friesland cows and a bull that was the joy of Mr Van der Walt's heart. He bred a few riding-horses too – Basuto ponies.

Wild ostriches roamed in the paddocks, white egrets were always near the flocks and sat on the broad backs of the cattle feasting on ticks and other parasites, secretary birds stalked through the grain in search of snakes, waterfowl haunted the dams, and after the rains, tall storks descended on the green lucerne lands and fed off Karoo caterpillars.

I fell more and more deeply in love with Springbok Spruit season by season, year by year. As a child, as an adolescent, as a young woman, that lonely Karoo farm stole my heart. Rita loved it too, but only because it was home. She was a pretty child, golden-haired like her brother, inclined to preen herself in front of every mirror she could find. She was curiously sophisticated for a country bred girl and had no deep feeling for the land.

Kobie was steeped in it. Every grain of earth and blade of grass, every bush and bird and beast was significant to him. He taught me to see many aspects through his eyes, riding across the veld, climbing the koppies or strolling down to the big dam in the evening when shy springbok joined the cattle at the water's edge. The sheep had their own drinking places and did not come to the big dam. We'd watch the blue cranes standing one-legged in the shallows and see the wild geese and ducks flighting back from their feeding grounds in immaculate V formation.

'Squadrons,' Kobie said. 'They know not to get in each other's way. Listen to the finks twittering in the rushes and the yellow weaver-birds kicking up a shindy round their nests.'

'Such beautiful tidy nests —'

He laughed, blue eyes mischievous.

'They're like you and your tree-house. The female bullies the male till he gets the nest just right for her. "Not that way, man – *this* way!" All that palaver you hear now is bird women nagging their mates.'

We'd watch the tremendous panoply of the Karoo sunset, silent and awed, as the ever-changing lagoons of crimson, gold and purest jade lit the western sky, flinging far-reaching reflections on to rock and crag in fiery splendour and washing the veld with the soft delicate pink of flamingo feathers.

At those times my whole being was flooded by a strange, almost pleasurable, melancholy, a sense of infinity, a fore-knowledge of love with all its joy and anguish and of the sad brevity of a moment of intense beauty vanishing in the vast wastes of eternity.

Dusk falls fast after sundown and high on the slope above the dam we'd see the lights prick orange squares in the homestead. As they glowed above us we'd guess who'd entered the lighted rooms of the big tin-roofed house with its fly-wired stoeps.

'That'll be Annie laying the table in the dining-room. Boy, am I hungry!'

Kobie was always hungry – especially at Springbok Spruit where everything tasted so much better than it did in the town.

Mrs Van der Walt was a wonderful cook and she liked to see us tuck into her lavish meals.

'You have to grow big and strong – most of all, you, Jo! You're a little grasshopper, light and quick, nothing to get hold of – just a chirrup and a spring in the sunshine.'

Rita was quite sturdy then. It was only later, that she set about getting thin and keeping that way. Kobie was a boxer and a rugger player, a fine swimmer and runner and useful on the tennis court. He expended endless energy and had to put it back. All of us drank glasses of rich Friesland milk last thing at night.

I was a little shy of Mr Van der Walt at first. He was tall and powerful with a blond beard and bright blue eyes as laughing as his son's, but soon I got used to his teasing. Mrs Van der Walt was tall too, with a plaited coronet of red-gold hair. She walked like a queen or a Bantu woman carrying a water calabash on her head, and she treated me kindly in the same easy-going manner she used towards her own children. She taught me to ride, and to swim in the lovely swimming-pool near the house and, when she was satisfied that I could manage on my own, she put me in Kobie's charge.

'Take care of Jo. These are new things to her – riding and swimming – and she could get into difficulties. I trust her to you, Kobie.'

'Okay, Ma,' he said.

He meant it too. Oh, Kobie, where did we go so terribly wrong – you and I?

What season did I love most at Springbok Spruit – spring, summer, autumn or winter? Winter, I think. I can smell it now – the dry aromatic veld – and feel the cutting edge of the clean sharp air when snow lay deep and shining white on the long mauve range of the Sneeuberg. I can see the frost crystals spangled on spiders' webs across the low bush and the steamy morning breath of our snorting ponies as we galloped into the new day. At night Rita and I had a wood and candlebrush fire in our room. It was wonderfully snug when the wind outside wailed round the house. Now and again we'd shiver and cuddle down under our eiderdowns as the grunt of a leopard or the hunting call of a jackal, *yaa-ya-ya*, threatened the sheep. But we were warm and we were safe, and we whispered and giggled till sleep overcame us. When we woke the silvery wood-ash was still warm in the hearth. It was never swept away in winter, it was the foundation of the fire to come.

Rita and I developed an intimate friendship born of propinquity and the ties that gradually began to bind me more and more closely to her brother.

Kobie, being the boy and a year older than we were, was the natural leader in all our escapades. He was affectionate, impulsive and merry but often inclined to be aggressive. He showed off for me, and later he fought for me. Even then, when we were not yet teenagers, I had boyfriends at school – mostly English-speaking – and Kobie detested them. This pleased me.

Verfontein primary school was, of course, a government school and 'mother tongue education' was compulsory, so the Van der Walts were taught in the Afrikaans section and I was instructed by English-speaking teachers. It was co-educational and about seventy per cent of the pupils were Afrikaans. In the coastal cities and Johannesburg the ratio would have been the other way. The playground was moody. Sometimes the children mixed, at others they played in their own language group. Kobie was gregarious and hardy. A rough game or a dust-up and he'd be in the thick of it. Only too often he came home with a black eye or a bloody nose. He made no excuses.

'All boys fight,' said Daddy easily. 'It's the nature of the human beast.'

Mummy shook her head. She knew the playground of Verfontein primary school by long experience and close observation.

'It's not the usual pattern. This one fights with his own.'

'What does she mean?' I asked Rita. I guess we were about nine or ten then.

Rita's blue eyes met mine with ancient wisdom. 'Kobie fights mostly with Afrikaans boys.'

'Why? Why should he do that?'

'Because they tease him.'

35

'What about?'

'Having 'n Engelse nooi.'

'An English sweetheart, me?'

'Ja. You, Jo.'

So, even then, I began to think of him in a different way. The black eye and the bloody nose were a sort of tribute to me. In a way I was proud, but sometimes I was frightened. If another boy wanted to carry my satchel for me or walk home with me Kobie found some reason to head him off – with a punch, if necessary.

A pattern was being established. But we were not even teenagers then. How could we know where it was leading?

❧ 4 ❧

WHEN KOBIE TURNED TWELVE HE LEFT US TO GO TO
the secondary school at Stellenbosch.

Stellenbosch is a beautiful Afrikaans educational centre in
the heart of the fruit-growing Western Cape. It combines
the old and the new with grace and dignity in the dappled
shade of magnificent oaks. Since the secondary school did
not take boarders Kobie was once again a lodger, this time
with the family of his maternal uncle, David Erasmus, professor of Anthropology at Stellenbosch University.

Professor and Mrs Erasmus had two teenage sons so
Kobie was no longer cock-of-the-roost as he'd been in our
home. But he was adaptable, plucky and volatile, and, if
he found that first term difficult, he didn't admit it.

In the following December Rita and I wrote our entrance
exams for our respective senior schools.

Rita was to go to Stellenbosch with her brother while I
was destined to be a boarder at St Catherine's, my mother's
old school in Cape Town.

For six years we three had been inseparable. I was desolate.
Rita would still have Kobie in the new life, I would be on
my own with strangers in a strange setting.

'You'll have Gran near you – her flat at Muizenberg will be your home,' Mummy consoled me.

I was fond of Mummy's mother and the thought of her being near comforted me. If only she weren't so deaf!

The day Mummy took me to St Catherine's was a zero in my life. After the homeliness of Verfontein this impressive school petrified me.

Miss Winters, the headmistress, was as brisk and patronizing with me as she was agreeable to Mummy.

'Your mother was head girl of St Catherine's in her last year,' she told me. 'You've quite a lot to live up to here, young Jo. Even if you did come top of your class at . . . Verfontein.'

The buildings and playing fields were hacked out of the lower slopes of Table Mountain and surrounded by pine and oak woods.

'It's shut in,' I whispered rather hysterically to Mummy. 'I don't like it. The mountain crushes me.'

'Nonsense, Jo!' She'd noted my reaction to St Catherine's with alarm. 'If the mountain makes you feel shut in, as you put it, you can look across the bay. What could be lovelier and brighter than all that sea and sky and the far blue mountains?'

More mountains, for heaven's sake! Mummy'd grown up at the Cape and she loved and often missed it, whereas I'd grown up on a vast empty plateau where hills and mountains varied, but never dominated, the scene, where they rose on the horizon in jacaranda blue ranges, soft as folded velvet,

between the clearer blue of the sky and the hazy lavender
of bush and African distance.

'You wait!' said Mummy. 'You'll fall in love with the
sea, Jo-Jo —'

'You don't have to sell me the sea,' I grumbled. 'The sea's
fine! But I hate old Table Mountain.'

She shrugged and looked sad and drawn as she kissed me
goodbye. She was afraid, I think, that I had already begun
to identify St Catherine's and all that it stood for with the
most forbidding aspects of its surroundings.

On my first night at the school I so irrationally feared and
hated, nature physically confirmed the emotional turmoil of
the day. Fortunately I was prepared, for Rita had beaten me
to it in the race for maturity. So, when the new strange pain
woke me and doubled me up, I guessed the reason. At last
I was a woman!

Perhaps my feeling of an altered status helped me to feel
less of a minnow in the big pond of St Catherine's. In that
respect, at least, I was one up on several of the new girls
whose dormitory I shared.

My bed was near a window looking out upon the grim
old mountain. Often the straight massive silhouette against
the summer sky was obscured by a snow-white cascading
cloth of cloud. I always expected it to engulf St Catherine's
but somehow it never did and we played our cricket or
tennis with the wind blowing us off our feet, its monstrous
tumult forcing us to shriek at each other to be heard. It
lashed the forests and whipped up the bay, tearing boats

from their moorings. Even great liners were unable to enter harbour till the south-easter abated.

Mrs Browning, my grandmother, was a widow. She lived alone in a spacious flat just across the road from the sea. She was fond of me and kind, but at first I reckoned she wasn't much of a companion. Her deafness and silliness with her hearing-aid scrambled the lines of communication between us. She'd grown used to living in a world of her own and I realize now that it must have been an effort for her to include me. She did so valiantly.

One Sunday, towards the end of my first term at St Catherine's, Kobie and Rita came all the way from Stellenbosch to spend the day. Gran and I met them at Cape Town station. Gran drove her own car – rather slowly and carefully – and she always heard better in the car. The vibration helped, she said. I was excited at seeing my friends again, but at first we were all three a little reserved. And Gran couldn't help being a bit of a spanner in the works. As soon as we got back to the flat it was clear that we were in for one of those days when her hearing-aid was unco-operative. When she turned it up to full strength we could all hear it crackle and she winced as she reduced the volume.

'The noises this damn thing makes are deafening,' she grumbled.

'*Deafening*?' murmured Rita. I caught the twinkle in her eye.

Gran kept asking Kobie and Rita questions, missed out on the answers, and came up with remarks that were way off the beam. Somehow this made me feel a fool. And of course she talked too much. Mummy used to say Gran talked the hind leg off a donkey because it was easier than listening.

When the three of us went to the beach in the afternoon Rita said:

'It's hard on your ouma, being so deaf —'

'It's hard on everybody,' grinned Kobie. 'I felt a real clot having to shout at her. Nothing I said was worth bawling at the poor thing. But, my goodness, that cookie of your ouma's certainly gave us a wonderful dinner!'

Kobie had had two helps of everything and Gran's eyes had been out on stalks watching him tuck in, but Maria, Gran's faithful coloured maid, who was wearing red boots, a purple dress and her best wig, really appreciated his appetite.

'Maria's a marvellous cook,' I said, 'And Gran prefers her bright colours to uniforms. She says it's like having a parakeet in the flat.'

We lay in the lee of the gaily-painted bathing-boxes. The fine silver-white sand was warm and silky against our bare bodies. Kobie was stealing glances at me because I filled the tiny bra of my bikini nicely now, though the rest of me was still narrow and boyish. I envied Rita's fuller curves. Kobie had grown much taller. He was muscular and strong, with the long powerful legs and deep chest of an athlete. I liked his close-fitting ears, a little pointed at the top like a faun's.

Once we were alone the restraint between us slackened and soon we were chattering away about the Erasmus home in Stellenbosch where Kobie and Rita were happy enough with their uncle and aunt and cousins – though Oom Dawie was evidently a dry stick. I had my turn too, letting off steam about St Catherine's, where I still felt unsettled.

'It's not the work – I can manage the work all right – and I like the games. It's the wind and that mountain looming right over the place. We go for walks in the woods to collect botanical specimens and we plough through dead pine-needles and oak leaves. Imagine the leaves falling already!'

'The oaks are always out of step,' said Kobie. 'They moult too soon and sprout before the winter's over.'

'You're just missing the open spaces of the Karoo,' said Rita. 'I miss them too. But we've got all that for holidays. It's really people who count. Nothing in life counts as much as people. What are the other girls like?'

'Not too bad.'

Kobie said: 'You don't sound keen.'

'I mean, can you get along with them?' asked Rita, who had a natural understanding of the essential things of life. What in the world could be more important than the ability to get along with other human beings? I doodled in the sand with a fastidious forefinger, my face hidden by the long fall of my hair.

'Sure. I've got friends —'

'And their brothers,' she suggested mischievously.

'Well, there's one – a Rhodesian. His sister often brings him here on Sundays. It's lonely for them at boarding-school so far from home.'

'Is he good-looking? Tall and dark —'

'All that.'

'What age?'

'Seventeen.'

'Aha! A *man!* Girls go for dark men.' She threw a sidelong glance at her brother who scowled at her. 'Is he your special, Jo-Jo?' she asked.

I wasn't answering that. I sprang up.

'Come, let's go in the sea!'

We raced across the beach and plunged madly into the waves, laughing and ducking each other with Rita and me ganging up on Kobie.

'Man, we haven't got *this* in the Karoo!' he gasped at last.

We were surfing without boards, stimulated by the sea and the exercise. We threw ourselves into the bursting rollers – breasting them, riding them, diving through them to come up in the vast heaving Indian Ocean beyond the breakers. Then we'd swim quietly around, waiting for the perfect wave. We'd see the long swell rise, steep and formidable, clear green, beginning to curl at the top, white mane flying.

'Oh boy, this is it!'

We'd fling ourselves down the shining avalanche of water with perfect timing, feeling the crest break on our backs, submerging us in surf, bearing us up and shorewards, breathless and glowing. We were no longer our separate selves; we were as elemental as the sea itself, part of it and of each other.

Afterwards we lay behind the bathing-box where we'd left our towels. Sand adhered to our tingling salt-wet skin or dusted off lightly as the sun dried us. We were prone and silent, touched by brief languor. I lay on my back, half

43

sleepy, wholly desirous, aware of Kobie in a new exciting way. His eyes, under the thick lowered lashes, were exploring my smooth near-naked body as if they were hands, gentle but eager, stroking, discovering, lingering, enjoying. Were they trembling? No, it was I whose nerves were tingling under the touch of those phantom hands.

5

AFTER THE PERIOD OF ADJUSTMENT WAS OVER I
settled down quite well at St Catherine's for a while. Another
thing, the more I came to know my grandmother the fonder
I became of her. We both began to look forward to our
Sundays together, even in winter when she and I would walk
for miles along the beach at low tide. She used a stick on
those walks because at times she'd feel giddy. Then she'd
pause for a while to let the spell pass.

'I had an operation we hoped might cure my deafness,'
she explained in one of those pauses. 'It didn't work and this
dizziness is the result. I've learnt to live with it.'

'When was the op, Gran?'

She flapped a gaunt hand vaguely. 'Oh, long long ago
when I was a young woman. I've never been allowed to
swim since then. A pity. I used to love to surf – just as you
do.'

'When you were young!' Till then I'd associated her deafness with old age. She smiled.

'Oh, it's not only old people who are hard of hearing,
Jo-Jo. In certain cases childbirth increases the tendency.
That's what happened to me.'

The wind had risen; it smelt of rain and salt spray. 'We're

45

going to be caught in a storm,' she added. 'We must hurry home. I'm all right now.'

Gran could walk me off my feet. She leaned into the approaching storm and we headed homewards in companionable silence. I was fourteen then, and I'd long since overcome my early embarrassment at having to speak up in her company. Of course, it was easier for us to talk when we were alone together. Then she'd watch my face attentively. She was good at lip-reading.

Her flat had become my second home, and her coloured help, Maria, was an even better friend to me than our Verfontein Lizzie. Maria had a smooth-looking boyfriend and a passion for dancing. Saturday was her dancing night and the wonder is that she never seemed to have a hangover when she cooked our Sunday lunch, which was always extra good for my sake. My Rhodesian schoolfriend, Selma Lavis, and her brother Charles, often shared the feast. Gran liked me to treat the flat as my home. So did Maria. They were both inclined to tease me about Charles. With some reason.

Quite often, when his sister accepted a Sunday invitation that didn't appeal to him, he came to the flat on his own. Then, after surfing, we'd relax in the lee of the dunes and get to know each other in a new way. A touch, a look, the stimulus of the sea, the warmth of the sunbaked sand and I'd find myself guessing at undiscovered worlds of sensuous excitement.

'I s'pose, in your home town . . . Verfontein . . . you've got a boyfriend?'

We were both breathless. There'd been brine in the taste of his kisses.

I answered his question with another.

'So you have a girlfriend at home?'

He grinned. 'Like the migrant Bantu labourer who expects to have a city-wife here and a tribal-wife in his own territory to plough his land and see his small son herds the cattle?'

'Wife? Well, that'd be a bit much at your age! But I guess there's a girl near your father's ranch —'

'Just like there's a boy waiting for you on a Karoo sheep farm . . . Why, Jo, you're blushing! Well, never mind, our homes are far away. Meanwhile, there's here and now and you and me.'

I fell half in love with Charles Lavis that summer – perhaps a little more than half – but when Selma asked me to spend the June holidays in Rhodesia, I made excuses. I found that I was homesick for Verfontein . . . and Springbok Spruit. In some inexplicable way, Charles – dark, shaggy, unconventional and artistic – had 'lighted me up' for Kobie. I realize now that he treated my youth with chivalry and forbearance. I daresay that's why Gran liked him. She trusted him.

I lost touch with Charles the following year when he left school in Cape Town and went to Rhodes University in Grahamstown. For a while I missed him very much.

I was fifteen when St Catherine's gave me my first disappointing report. I'd gone home for the winter holidays. I knew that my schoolwork had fallen off and when I sat with my parents by the fire on the evening of my arrival and Daddy studied my report I was nervous. His thick black hair had greyed and his humorous deeply lined face was sombre as he passed the report to Mummy. She spread it under the reading lamp. I saw her brows draw together and her mouth tighten.

'English "excellent",' she said at last. 'Every other subject "fair" or "disappointing". Your form mistress remarks "Jo's work this term is below her normal high standard. She must give up day-dreaming and concentrate more."'

'Why this . . . disappointing work, Jo?' asked Daddy.

'I don't know, Daddy.'

'Day-dreaming . . . This is hardly the time in your school career for day-dreaming. You write your exams at the end of this year —'

I was upset and temperamental, unaccustomed to scholastic failure.

'All right, rub it in! It's also getting near my last year when Mummy hoped I'd be head girl. I'm not made of the right material. I'd hate to be head girl!'

'Take it easy, Jo,' Mummy said quietly. 'We just want to know why the . . . day-dreaming?'

I made a confused attempt to excuse myself.

'Honestly, I can't explain. Sometimes, when I'm listening to the teacher, I sort of . . . lose it . . . and, if you lose a bit, you can't quite catch up, you start to think about something else —'

'You're thinking about something else in the first place,' said Mummy severely, 'that's the real trouble.'

48

It wasn't. The real trouble was so insidious that none of us ever guessed at it then.

I promised to try harder and to do better next term.

The best part of that holiday was the week I spent at Springbok Spruit. The Van der Walts were as warm-hearted and hospitable as ever. Nobody there knew about my bad report and nobody gave school a thought. There was so much else to occupy our attention.

One evening Kobie and I walked our ponies back to the stables after a hard cross-country gallop. It was nearly dark and lights were already glowing gold in the windows of the old homestead, warm and welcoming. All round us in the dusk we could hear the invisible life of the veld waking and stirring. With sunset the temperature had plummeted. Old Koos, the coloured groom, had gone to his home some distance away. Dogs barked down there among the labourers' cottages and someone twanged a guitar.

We put our ponies to bed ourselves, unsaddling them, rubbing them down, and hanging up the bridles. The stable smelt of hay and leather and warm horse. We fed them carrots and felt their supple, silky lips in the flat of our palms. We were filled with love for our dear Basuto ponies – so gentle, strong and sure-footed – and then Kobie's arms were round me and we were filled with love for each other. It wasn't passionate at first, it was all-pervasive.

Then it wasn't all-pervasive any more but strictly personal, because Kobie's hands were under my woolly sweater, on my warm body, and every bit of me was changing, melting, tingling and making its own sharp burning responses to those ardent hands and lips, to the strength of his limbs, the hard pressure of his body. He was sixteen and a man, less subtle and controlled than Charles Lavis, already more demanding.

'No, Kobie! Not like this – not here.'

What was I saying? What was I promising? My mouth was dry, my words stifled by his lips over mine. It was almost dark in the stable, and somewhere near by, the plant supplying the farm with electricity was pulsing. Everything was pulsing, even the air about us. The horses stamped in their stalls, the sound of their hooves muffled by sawdust. A bridle clanged faintly on its hook as my shoulder touched the shining snaffle. I leaned against the wall and tried to push Kobie from me, but he stood, resolute, just holding me to him, his face buried in my hair, the long sigh of his breath warm on my scalp. After a while he said:

'I love you and you belong to me – even if you aren't all mine yet —'

'I'm yours – I have been ever since I can remember . . .'

The friendly twilight, the untroubled movements of the ponies and the hum and throb of the dynamo in the adjacent engine-house held us in a quiet spell. I was very still in Kobie's embrace, my face against his chest, hearing the thump of his heart, steady and strong, but fast. His voice was tense when he spoke the words I can never forget. There, in the safe peace of the leather-smelling gloom, I knew with a shiver of premonition that he meant what he said.

'If any man takes you from me, Jo, I'll kill him.'

6

IN THE FOLLOWING YEAR KOBIE WAS ENROLLED AT
the University of Cape Town and we were once again
within easy reach of each other.

U.C.T. is English-speaking. It is quite usual in South
Africa for English-speaking families to send their sons to an
Afrikaans-speaking university and vice versa.

'When we get married,' Kobie said to me once, 'I guess
we'll speak more English than Afrikaans in our home.'

'Will you mind that?'

'Of course not. It's a world language. Essential. Afrikaans
may be the mother tongue of the majority of white South
Africans, but it's not much use to us anywhere else. Except
perhaps, Belgium and Holland.'

Rita, of course, was still at Stellenbosch swotting for her
matric – as I was supposed to be doing at St Catherine's.

On principle, no student does much work in his first
university year, just as no senior in her senses idles away her
last school terms with the hurdle of final exams ahead. So
the timing was bad for me. But we didn't care. Kobie had
acquired a little souped up Mini-Cooper and whenever I got
my head out of my books and could find some excuse to slip
out of 'prison', we were off and away.

Gran didn't see much of me that summer. I think she missed me but every now and again we showed up at the Muizenberg flat and tucked into one of Maria's magnificent meals. That bird of bright plumage understood very well that I had reached the age of special boyfriends, but Gran felt it necessary to remind me that my parents would not expect me to fail matric.

Apart from my studies, there was a golden quality about that summer and the lovely bright autumn that followed. Kobie taught me to drive on deserted country roads and we discovered the breathtaking beauty of the Cape. We climbed the mountains I had once found oppressive, and, from high pinnacles, we saw that the oceans were far vaster than the veld, Atlantic to the west, Indian to the east. We made love under the sky, like Pagans. Unlike our own empty Karoo, the Peninsula was full of secret places shaded by great trees, and lonely coves and beaches, and white dunes that smoked softly when the wind blew. Kobie loved the sonorous murmur of the sea.

'Being so much with Gran at Muizenberg, I'm more used to it than you are,' I said. 'I hardly notice it now.'

In winter, when the rainy north-westers blustered, we liked to watch the huge Atlantic rollers bursting against the cliffs where long ago the sailing ships of Portuguese, Dutch and English mariners had been broken on the pitiless rocks of the Cape of Storms. Afterwards there was the refuge of his warm room.

Kobie had been unable to get into Smuts Hall, the men's residence, but he had a bedsitter and shower in the house of a widow who lived in Rosebank, near the university. It was like a tiny bachelor flat with its own garden entrance and he could park the Mini-Cooper outside in the drive. Mrs Malherbe, his landlady, was a friend of Professor and Mrs Erasmus and she was used to students. She gave her lodger no food, but he had an electric kettle, toaster and saucepan, so he could scratch up a meal for himself when necessary. Her maid cleaned the room every day except Sundays. I didn't have to be back at school till eight on Sunday evenings, so we could make ourselves toast and ham and scrambled eggs and heat some soup for an early supper.

'In some ways, you're better off here than in residence,' I said, selfish and possessive.

'So right, cookie.'

I cracked the eggs into the melted butter in the saucepan and added a dash of milk, salt and pepper. The toast popped up and he took it out and buttered it. He said:

'It's like being a little bit married. But not enough. Listen, Jo, getting university degrees is a long business. I won't be in a position to marry for years. I don't fancy that.'

'It won't be too bad. It isn't as if I were going to varsity too. I'll do a crash business course and get my speeds in six months and then I'll get a job and a tiny pad of my own. Or I could team up with Rita if she doesn't get into one of the women's residences —'

'She probably will. She's mad to do art and drama and it's much better for her to live in and share varsity life fully – work, play, social, the lot.'

'Do *you* share it fully enough?'

'Naturally. Especially now the rugger season's begun. But I still say you and I can't go on like this for years and years —'

'Let's drift, Kobie. We're so very young . . .'

Kobie was part of me and of my whole existence and I never doubted that I loved him, yet I couldn't help remembering the way I had responded to Charles Lavis – my adolescent body craving his touch. Now, suddenly, the permanence and finality of the idea of marriage frightened me. It would be the ultimate seal upon a love affair that was still fluid and irresponsible. Yet Kobie's assumption that we would marry – and his impatience that we should – made me feel happy and safe. I knew he'd had girlfriends at Stellenbosch. He'd been frank about that – no names, of course. 'But it wasn't serious, it was just growing up, experimenting around – and that went for them too. You're the girl in my life, liefie – no one else.' *Liefie* – I was glad to be his 'little love,' the girl in his life.

Somehow I scrambled through matric with a mark or two to spare. I received the news in Verfontein in January and Daddy and Mummy were far from pleased.

'You can see,' I said defiantly, 'I'm not cut out for an academic career. It's a business college and a job for me.'

We were sitting on the side stoep in the hot summer twilight. The cicadas were shrilling, but less loudly, I thought, than in other summers.

'You've disappointed us,' said Mummy. 'You were bright enough at primary school.'

When I didn't answer she repeated what she had said, and

added, 'I'm sorry, Jo. But I think Miss Winters was right when she said you weren't keeping your mind on your work. You do a lot of wool-gathering these days.'

'There's another thing.' Daddy lit a cigarette, and in the process spilt Marmalade's successor out of his lap, a black kitten known as Inky, which instantly began to tease Honey's ears. Honey snapped. She had grown old and intolerant of feline playfulness. 'Another rather important thing. You've been talking about sharing a flat with Rita when you start your business course in Cape Town. Now, Mrs Van der Walt tells us Rita's managed to get into Baxter Hall Women's Residence, which is quite the best thing for her. She can be integrated into varsity life at once.'

'I know, Daddy. I know all about that. So I thought I'd find a tiny bachelor girl flat – in Cape Town maybe . . .'

'Jo-Jo! That simply won't do. You're only seventeen and we can't allow it —'

Mummy put in quickly, 'We can't afford it either. The farmers have had a bad season and that reflects in the town. When the farmers don't spend, Zebra Shopping Centre doesn't show a profit. Money is tight —'

'Well, what then?' I must have looked as anxious and suspicious as I felt, because there was a long pause while my parents exchanged significant glances. I was concentrating all right now, watching their expressions, waiting for it – whatever 'it' might be. And, when it came, how obvious it was! Mummy took the plunge.

'Gran wants you to stay with her. There's a good train service between Muizenberg and Cape Town. She'd have company and you'd have a comfortable home. She's a lonely person, Jo. She loves you. And the arrangement wouldn't cost anybody a cent, broadly speaking.'

I stared from one to the other. I was genuinely very fond of my grandmother, but this simply wasn't fair. Minutes passed in silence. Daddy threw his cigarette butt away and got up restlessly. He leaned against a slender cast-iron pillar and I couldn't see his face because it was dusk already and the house lights were not yet on. A bat flew to and fro in the garden. Mummy looked down at her hands and stroked her right wrist with her left thumb. She'd fractured her wrist once and it still worried her at times. I thought her fingers were ugly and blunt. Practical. My own were like my father's – long and nervous. At last I spoke hotly. My personal freedom – my whole conception of independent life – was at stake.

'I'm seventeen. Too young, you say, for a flat of my own! So you want me to *live* with my grandmother. Just the two of us. Has it struck you that I'm too young to be cooped up with somebody old and deaf?'

Mummy's head came up and she faced me reproachfully. Inside the house Lizzie had switched on the dining-room light to set the table for the evening meal; she didn't close the curtains and it fell full on Daddy's face. He looked shocked. The bat wheeled towards the light and the grapes, heavy on the pergola over our heads.

'That wasn't very kind, Jo,' Daddy said, quietly.

'It's true,' I flared, trembling, ashamed and angry. 'And what's more, I realize it's been pre-arranged between the three of you without one word to me. And if I dodge out now I'll hurt Gran terribly. All right then – let it stand for now. But when I'm in a job, earning my own money, I'll plan my life *my* way.'

I was on my feet, the pulses beating in my throat. Mummy controlled herself visibly.

'When you're earning your own money we'll discuss the next step. You'll find us reasonable, Jo. We don't want to curb your spirit. When you're eighteen we'll consider you . . . of age.'

'Even our enlightened government is prepared to do that!'

Daddy suddenly lost patience.

'Get your diploma – or whatever it is. Then we'll go from there.'

Well, I got that diploma and landed a job as secretary to the branch manager of an oil company.

It was summer again by then, and life at the sea was good. Talk of my leaving Gran was postponed. She was kind and generous and allowed me to go my own way. She took the situation between Kobie and me for granted and made him feel welcome at any time, and this welcome included Rita, who was studying Art and Drama at varsity. Gran never found it difficult to get on with Rita whose training was teaching her to speak clearly and expressively. Rita was fun too, good company.

She had grown into a beauty, as glowing and golden as a summer day with wide set sky-blue eyes – not laughing or stormy eyes like her brother's, reflecting his own moods and feelings, but clear and uncommitted till the part she had decided to play took charge and lit them with the attributes and fancies of some fictitious character. She was careful not to put on weight, resisting even Maria's most delicious dishes.

'I'm very nearly too tall for an actress,' she explained. 'I daren't get fat as well.'

'Haven't you a special boyfriend?' I asked her once.

She shook her head with a swirl of shining hair and laughed.

'Oh, no. I play the field. I want a career so I choose the boyfriends who can help it along. I s'pose one day I'll fall hook, line and sinker for somebody not remotely connected with stage, screen or T.V. Cross your fingers for me that I don't do anything so silly.'

When – years later – she did do something 'so silly' she still knew where she was going. The limelight was her guiding star.

While Rita was 'playing the field' I was becoming steadily more deeply involved with her brother.

I had my own latch-key. Gran slept soundly and our voices never disturbed her when he brought me home after some party or dance, but if we banged a door it woke her. Maria was no problem. She had her room across the quadrangle in the staff quarters of the flats, where life was often violent and dramatic. But even when the siren of a police van or ambulance wailed to a stop outside those little rooms across the yard Gran remained oblivious. With her hearing-aid on the bedside table she was insulated from interruption.

Even the ringing of her telephone bell failed to wake her – as we learned one fateful summer night.

It was a public holiday and Kobie and I had been out dancing. It was after midnight when we closed the front door of the flat softly behind us and my bedroom door even more carefully. The building was quiet, with only an isolated window here and there showing a light. Kobie whispered:

'Your gran's fast asleep. I can hear her grunting peacefully like a hippo.' We stifled our laughter.

My window was wide open to the fresh briny night. Coloured lights garlanded the children's playground across the road where a group of young people plucked at their guitars and sang folk songs. Phosphorus fired the long rollers under the moon and the surf thumped on the beach and sighed away with the ebb. The tang of salt and ozone filled the air. We stood at the window, inhaling great gulps of it. The mountains across the bay were insubstantial in the starlight.

The night breeze touched our bare bodies with its seaborne caress. We turned from the window and Kobie lifted me on to my bed. The carnival lights from the playground flickered over our lovemaking with harlequin enchantment, and it seemed to us, that magic night, that we could never bear to be parted.

Then the telephone bell rang. On and on and on.

At last I tore myself out of Kobie's embrace, pulled on a wrap and padded into the hall to answer the insistent summons. Enough to wake the dead – though my grandmother slept on, still puffing out her small hippo snorts from time to time. I picked up the receiver.

'Josephine Carter speaking. Who is it?'

The hall clock struck the half hour. One-thirty! Surely a wrong number?

But it was Rita, her voice choked and full of tears, ringing from Baxter Hall.

'Jo, is Kobie there? Daddy's been gored by the Friesland bull. He's in Verfontein Hospital —'

'Oh, Rita, Rita . . .'

Kobie was beside me, a towel round his middle, his curly fair hair on end, his eyes anxious. He took the receiver from me.

'Ritakie – I heard what you said to Jo. When did it happen? . . . This evening . . . We must go home at once . . . Ja, straight to Verfontein hospital. I'll fetch you right now. When did they ring you? . . . Nine o' clock. No, Ma couldn't have found me at Mrs Malherbe's. I wasn't there . . . You kept trying here? But you'd never raise Mrs Browning after eight o' clock. She goes to bed then and takes off her hearing-aid. A fire engine wouldn't disturb her . . .'

They had fallen into Afrikaans, Kobie's voice taut. I only heard his end of the conversation. When he hung up and turned to me his face was drawn and shocked, ghastly in the dimness of the hall lit only by the outside landing light shining through the frosted glass panel of the front door. He slumped on to the stool by the telephone table and his shoulders sagged.

'Pa . . . Critical, Rita says . . . What does that mean, Jo? That he's going to die?'

I moved to him and my wrap fell apart. I took his face and held it between my breasts and felt tears trickle on to my skin. I realised then that in all the years I had known him I had never seen him cry – not even as a child when he was defiant, bruised and bloody-nosed from fighting in the playground, not when he was scolded afterwards, not when he'd been given cuts for naughtiness, nor even on that first day when he and his sister were left by their mother in our home – two little strangers, unaccustomed to our ways and even our language. They must have felt abandoned. Rita had cried. I stroked his hair with gentle fingers and slowly a new emotion towards my lover welled up in me. In that moment of his grief and anxiety I knew the meaning of tenderness.

❧ 7 ❧

KOBIE AND RITA DROVE THROUGH THE NIGHT, PUSHING the Mini-Cooper to her maximum speed. They reached Verfontein when the sun was high. They were in time to see their father alive. To bid him goodbye.

That night Kobie 'phoned me and we talked for a long while.

'So you see,' he said at last, 'I'll have to give up varsity and go back to manage Springbok Spruit. It'll be mine now, liefie. I told Pa you and I meant to marry and he gave us his blessing. It was the last thing he did. We don't have to wait for years and years, Jo-Jo. I need you now – as soon as you can marry me.' He was so sure of me. Somehow it hurts now to remember how sure he was that I'd never let him down – much less harm him.

In the following spring, when Kobie had finished a short agricultural course, we were married in the Anglican Church in Verfontein. So soon after Kobie's father's death it was a quiet family wedding, and Gran came up attended by Maria.

Kobie was not quite twenty on our wedding day and I was eighteen, but our parents made no objections. They knew that a farmer needs a wife and a good farm needs an

heir and it had long been understood that one day Kobie and
I would marry.

You take a good deal for granted when you're very young.
I'm not old now, God knows, but I've had plenty of time
to think, and I can see that my mother-in-law must sometimes have found it irksome when her impulsive inexperienced son took over Springbok Spruit, assisted – fortunately
– by the shrewd grizzled Afrikaans foreman, Jannie Bosman,
who'd grown up on the farm and was old enough to be
Kobie's father.

Afrikaners have a strong sense of family unity, especially
in the country, and it seemed perfectly natural to all of us
that we should move into the homestead with Ma.

Springbok Spruit had a reputation for hospitality and we
often had weekend house parties. Our town friends enjoyed
the riding, swimming, tennis and relaxation, and from time
to time Rita drove up from the Cape with some new boyfriend or another. Of course Ma continued to be mistress of
the house and Annie, the cook, had her own ways of making
it clear that she took her orders from the *die ounooi* – the old
mistress – and not from the young bride who had for years
been a child in this home. At times I resented her attitude
and grumbled to Kobie who only grinned and said:

'Leave well alone, liefie. Don't interfere.'

'Interfere! But this is my home as well as Ma's. Why can't
I put *my* stamp on it too?'

'It's Ma's home till she dies. Only after that does the house
come to us.'

Ma produced the solution herself. We had been out to the

far paddocks to see the autumn lambs and as Kobie drove us back to the homestead, he said:

'When the spring lambs are running with the ewes, there'll be a baby at Springbok Spruit, Ma. You'd better get your knitting needles flashing.'

She turned to me where I sat in the back seat, her face shining.

'Jo! What wonderful news.'

That night by the fireside she said:

'You two should build your own house. This homestead is my background – it's not Jo's. She has a right to have her home just the way she wants it – especially with a baby coming.'

I leaned forward eagerly, feeling my cheeks flush in the firelight. 'Oom Paul Joubert, over the hill, has two Italian builders fixing up alterations to his place. Perhaps —'

'Just so! They'll be through with that job in about a month. Then they could tackle a house for you. You needn't be in any hurry to leave me. Have your baby in Verfontein, Jo, and then bring him or her back here to the homestead and only move in to your own place later on when you feel up to coping with a family.'

So, in the months that followed, the shell of our home grew on the grassy site at the foot of the slope, from where you could see across the big dam and the veld to the Sneeuberg, capped with snow in the sparkling cold of mid winter. Kobie drove me to Johannesburg for a few days' shopping and we bought furniture and fittings and gay chintzes and rugs, and all the things we'd need for a nursery. After our baby was born we planned to finish our interior decorating. Then we'd move in. Our spring garden was already set out.

Sure enough, in September when the young merinos were frolicking and springbok lambs added their enchantment, our daughter was born in Verfontein hospital – a doll of a tiny girl, Mary Margerita, named for my mother and for Rita. We were crazy about her. Plenty of time for boys later on!

We took her back to the homestead. Her cradle was placed in Kobie's dressing-room adjoining our bedroom and the door was always kept open at night between the two rooms. She slept well. Remarkably quietly, I thought, though Kobie didn't agree with me.

'She makes puppy noises,' he said. 'Little snufflings. Ag, she's a lollipop!'

It was never Mary Margerita who woke me for her morning feed, it was the fullness of my own breasts warning me that it was six o' clock. I'd only hear her little grizzlings when I lifted her from the pretty frilly cradle.

She was just over a month old when I went into the dressing-room as usual and opened the curtains to let in the dawn light. Then I turned to the cradle, longing to pick up my warm cuddly baby.

Mary Margerita lay strangely still, not waxen pale as babies often are in sleep, but darkly mottled. No pouting lips and little sucking sounds to say she was awake and hungry, no movements of tiny hands and kicking feet. I bent down to lift her out of her cradle, but as I touched the little body, always so warm, my hands were frozen and paralysed by her ice-cold rigidity.

I shrieked then. 'Kobie! Kobie! She's ... *dead* ...'

In a moment he was beside me, his big strong hand over the tiny chest, feeling for the heartbeat that had ceased some time during the hours of darkness.

We stared at our child and at each other, dry-eyed, shaking with shock. Unbelieving, uncomprehending. What had happened? What could possibly have happened? We clung together.

'A snake ...' I whispered at last.

'There hasn't been a snake in this house – ever. In the garden, yes – here, no. Some sort of fit?'

'She had a bit of a chill yesterday, nothing to speak of ...'

We were so inexperienced. So helpless.

Afterwards the doctor explained that this could happen.

'She had a little cold, you say. Very slight, I know. But an infant can choke in its sleep. This is more common than you'd suppose.'

'But surely I'd have heard her!' I cried. 'The door was open between the two rooms.'

'Your husband heard nothing, Jo. It might have been a very small sound – hardly a sound at all.'

'Kobie sleeps deeply. He's out all day in the open air. But I'm her *mother*! It's inconceivable that I didn't hear my baby when she needed me.'

He shook his head. 'The young sleep soundly, my dear. Even the maternal instinct takes a rest.'

We didn't guess. Even then we didn't realize the thing that was happening to me. It was so gradual, so insidious, it had been creeping up on me since the days at St Catherine's when my teachers found me 'dreamy and inattentive'.

Our baby had choked to death unheard. I was going deaf.

8

RITA CAME HOME FOR CHRISTMAS.

By then we had moved into our new house. She was enthusiastic about it, but I was lethargic, more and more inclined to creep into my shell. She did her best to draw me out.

'You've had a traumatic experience, Jo. But you have to live again – for Kobie's sake. For Ma's – and for your own. You brood too much.'

'I blame myself —'

'Don't be silly! Come, let's play a set of tennis – sweat some weight off me. Oh, this Christmas overeating!'

She was determined to keep very thin. Her entire purpose was directed towards a successful stage career.

I think Ma was often anxious about her daughter. We knew that Rita ran around with a very bohemian crowd at varsity.

'Universal love is our creed,' she told us, partly to tease her mother whose disapproving expression amused her. 'Make love, not war – and do your own thing.'

'What's your thing, Ritakie?' asked Kobie. 'Not drugs, I hope.'

'No. I've tried a trip or two on this and that, but invariably finished up with an almighty hangover. I guess I'm allergic to drugs.'

'Thank God for that, at any rate.'

She delighted in shocking her audience and then pretending her description of life among her fellow students was just an act, but I suspected that most of what she said was only too true.

One hot evening, as we sat out on the stoep, Rita threw a searching glance at my drawn face and turned to her mother.

'I think Jo should take a holiday. Kobie too.'

'You're perfectly right,' agreed Ma. 'Jannie Bosman and I can run this place on our own for a while. What Kobie and Jo need is to get right away.' She turned to her son. 'Kobie, you remember that nice young couple – the Burtons from West Australia? They stayed with us here the year before you were married. They wanted to study our methods of sheep breeding —'

'Yes, of course I do. Jack and Jennie. You've met them here, Jo. They own a fine merino stud themselves. They asked me to visit them —'

'Then take Jo to Australia,' said Ma firmly. 'Fix it – and *soon*!'

That warm summer night, when we lay together in our big bed with the window wide open and the fragrance of the thorn flowers so sweet in the soft air, he drew me into his arms and said:

'They're right – Ma and Rita. We can't mourn for ever, liefie. Life goes on. There's all the future for both of us.'

All the future? It seemed so then. We'd begun to make plans – to live again.

The wind that rose and stirred our curtains blew the seeds of the Karoo acacias far and wide; and for us too seeds were sown – seeds of life and death.

In late January we made the long but comparatively easy flight from Johannesburg to Perth across the Indian Ocean, only touching down once at the mountainous green island of Mauritius.

Jack and Jennie Burton were at Perth airport to meet us at four in the morning. Jack was a good deal older than we were – about thirty-five with a slouchy walk, a spare figure and one of those lantern-jawed Australian faces. His wife was about thirty – casual and exotic, a painter who had already made quite a name for herself in artistic circles.

'We're not taking you straight to Sun Downs,' said Jack. 'We thought you'd like a few days here first, just to see something of Perth and its surroundings. We have a flat at Claremont on the riverside and we often come to town for a weekend.'

'We've left our two little girls at Sun Downs with Elsie McBride, our Scottish housekeeper and my brother, Rob,' Jennie explained. Rob's a surgeon in Sydney. Whenever he needs a break he comes to Sun Downs. And when I want to kick my heels I fly to Sydney. Ah, there's a city for you!'

Jack turned off the highway towards the lovely sweep of the Swan River between grassy banks and wooded cliffs and parked in the open garage under the small block of flats.

Sky and water were streaked with the cobweb silver of first light.

'Listen!' Jack pointed to a tall tree. 'The kookaburras. Laughing.'

'Good heavens, those birds really do laugh their ruddy heads off!' Kobie turned to me. 'Don't they, Jo? Have you ever heard anything like it?'

I shook my head and smiled. But it was only afterwards I knew what he'd said or that kookaburras 'laugh their ruddy heads off'. I was deaf from the plane – so I thought. It would wear off.

But it didn't wear off. Later that day I came out with it – the latent fear that was beginning to haunt me.

We woke round lunchtime after the deep sleep of travellers' exhaustion. I bathed my face and showered and began to revive. Kobie called something from the bedroom. When I didn't hear at first, he repeated his remark with a touch of irritation. I stood in the doorway between the shower and our room.

'Kobie, this deafness . . . from the plane? Is it really that? Or is it more – much more?'

Perhaps the fear was in my eyes, for he jumped up and came to me quickly, cool in the air-conditioned room, and I felt his arms encircle my naked body. He rocked me against him as if I were a child to be consoled.

'Forget it, liefie. It'll pass. Flying is often bad for ears.'

I let myself be comforted. But the shadow stayed in the back of my mind. Kobie too was afraid for me – for both of us. He'd held me as if to protect me from some intangible enemy too subtle and powerful to be kept at bay by a pair of human arms, however strong and loving.

Midsummer in Australia is fiercer than in South Africa. The sun stronger, the sky bluer, the beaches more dazzling. But uphill downdale Perth and its surroundings are softly green to counteract the glare – grass sidewalks, shady flowering trees, forested hills, and parks where the wild flowers grow in profusion. A few skyscrapers.

In the afternoon we lazed on the beach and swam in that glittering sea, the same Indian Ocean that washed our sands at Muizenberg.

Back at the garden-flat we had our sundowners on the terraced lawn above the river.

Our host and hostess were friendly and informal and I felt the terrible tension of the past few months begin to slacken. Kobie caught my eye often and smiled. I knew that he was happy to see me 'unwinding'.

'We thought you'd be tired tonight,' said Jennie, 'so we're eating at home. Any time we like.'

I didn't hear the footfall on the grass, only Jennie's sudden exclamation of surprise as a tall young man in his middle twenties bent over her light garden chair and kissed her on the cheek. His strong-featured face was bronzed in the sunset, his hands on her shoulders were long-fingered with well-kept nails. A lock of black hair fell across his brow.

'Rob! You were going to bury yourself in medical books this weekend!' She turned to us. 'Jo and Kobie, meet my brother, Rob Stirling.'

'Of course I've heard all about you both.' His voice was warm and deep, his smile lit and narrowed his hazel eyes. He looked at me as if he really saw me – and liked what he saw. For some reason I recalled Charles Lavis and Rita's schoolgirl taunt at Kobie – 'Girls go for dark men.' This one was magnetic.

'We've heard about you too,' grinned Kobie, 'but we thought you were away in the bundu, studying.'

'So I was, but I reckoned I was getting stale, so I came roaring down in Jack's Fiat Sports. Fast work! Hope you don't mind, Jack.'

'Does her good to give her a burn. Now we've got the Cessna, the Fiat doesn't get enough exercise.'

Rob handed his sister a piece of paper.

'Elsie's shopping list. The kids are fine. Elsie's good with them. They follow her around like puppies.'

'She's a gem,' agreed Jennie, putting the list in her bag. To us she added: 'Rob's planning to visit your part of the world one of these days. He's a buddy of the South African flying doctor in Lesotho and he has a pilot's licence. So he could be useful both as pilot and doctor.'

'Lesotho's not much farther from us than your Sun Downs is from here,' said Kobie. 'You'll have to include our farm in your plans, Rob.'

'Wonderful!' The young surgeon beamed. 'That's a promise.'

'Get yourself a beer, Rob, or whatever else you want,' said Jack. 'What about you, Kobie? A fill-up?'

Kobie and Rob strolled across the lawn and disappeared through the open French windows.

In the days that followed I made a great effort to pull my weight and join in everything to the full. It was easy enough when it was just ourselves, but the Burtons were popular, and, when they came to town, they were swept into a gay gang of friends. I found that my deafness 'from the plane' made it difficult to catch the names of the many strangers we met and the gist of conversation tossed quickly back and forth. In fact, I was glad when we left Perth and flew the four hundred miles north to Sun Downs with the Burtons in their Cessna. Rob drove up in the Fiat.

Sun Downs comprised about eighty thousand morgen of wheatlands and sheep paddocks and ran eight thousand sheep. The tawny summer grass, the windmills and wide horizon reminded me of the Transvaal veld. But there were other wholly Australian features. Groves of tall graceful pearly-barked ghost-gums in dry water-courses – and all those fantastic parrots! Colonies of grey and crimson galahs rested on T. V. aerials and eucalyptus trees, flocks of emerald 'twenty-eights' and clouds of exquisite little red-breasted rosellas flew around the grove of gums near the house, which was shaded by magnolias, willows, frangipanis and many other flowering trees and shrubs.

Elsie, the young housekeeper, was at the runway to meet us when the Cessna touched down, a little flaxen-haired girl bouncing up and down with excitement on either side of her. When they'd hugged their parents as if they'd been parted for years they were seized with sudden shyness. Jennie smiled down at them and then at us.

'Kobie and Jo, meet Elsie McBride. And these two littlies are our daughters, Pamela and Anna, aged four and three. We call Pamela Dimples.'

'I'm four and three quarters,' protested Dimples. 'Nearly five.'

Jack laughed. 'A woman's brief age of innocence, when every extra month adds importance and a little more privilege!'

We piled baggage and parcels into the waiting station-wagon and Jack drove us over to the house. As Kobie helped Jack take the bags indoors, I felt a soft little hand steal into mine. Dimples was looking up at me with a smile that accounted for her pet-name.

'Would you like to see our cubby?'

'I'd love to.' I'd no notion what a cubby was.

'Not now, darling,' said Jennie. 'Jo's tired. She'd probably like a sundowner.'

'But, Mom, it'll be too dark if we don't go at once.'

'That's true,' agreed Jack, and added to me: 'A cubby is a secret hide-out. You're being highly honoured, Jo.'

The two little girls led me through a rose garden at the height of its glory. A pretty little sheepdog, a kelpie, scampered ahead of us.

The cubby was tucked away between a huge palm and a bamboo thicket.

'It's completely hidden!' I said. 'I'd never have spotted it.'

'You're small,' said Dimples. 'You can get in. See, the roof's quite high.'

'When I was four and a half Kobie – my husband – made me a house in a tree. It was good, but not as good as this cubby. This is wonderful. Even a rush mat.' I knelt on the mat, the children next to me.

'Rob helped us build it,' said Anna, in a gabble of excitement. 'But a tree-house would be better. No grown-up could get into a house in a tree.'

'Rover couldn't either,' said Dimples. 'That would make him cross.'

Rover licked my face.

'Is he your watchdog?' I asked.

'Yes, and he likes you —'

'No wonder,' a deep voice remarked.

'Rob!'

His nieces sprang up and tore out to give him one of their exuberant greetings. Anna squealed with delight when he scooped her up, threw her into the air and caught her again.

'Dimples is too big to be treated like a rubber ball,' he explained, as he set Anna on her feet. 'I'm the rescue squad. I've been told to fetch you in for a drink, Jo.'

The little girls and the kelpie skipped ahead of us as we sauntered lazily through the rose garden. We paused to admire the delicate pink of Queen Elizabeth in full bloom. Then I saw that Rob was listening . . . entranced.

'At this time of evening and in the early mornings,' he said, 'the bird calls are at their best – the invitation and the response. Don't you love the variety? Just listen a moment.'

He was watching me intently, waiting for a comment, expecting me to pick out some particular call, to ask what bird was making it. I had no comments and no questions. I couldn't hear the birdsong any more than I'd heard the laughter of the kookaburras.

Rob Stirling was immensely observant. Diagnosis is a part of a doctor's mental equipment and Rob was no exception. In any case, I know now that his interest in me was personal, even then.

If I'm to seek truth in telling my story from A to Z then I'd better confess straight away that the moment Rob and I met there was that special flash between us, an electric current so powerful that we would have done well to keep out of range of each other! Kobie and I had grown side by side and very close over the years. Our marriage was solid, happy, and passionate too. Well-founded, not likely to be shaken by any passing infatuation, and I had no intention of allowing anything to disrupt it. I wanted no emotional or sexual entanglement. But Rob was as physically dangerous to me as a live rail. We both knew this and we both masked our knowledge. It wasn't easy because, as fellow guests of his sister and her husband, we were constantly thrown together in the islanded atmosphere of Jennie's lonely home set in its enchanted garden, wide parklands, wheatfields and pasturage.

Jack took Kobie around with him most days, for my husband was naturally interested in Sun Downs' superb stud and grain production in which human labour played a minimal part. Mechanization is the only solution to the vast scale of Australian agriculture and sheep and cattle breeding. Jennie spent hours in her studio and part of every morning giving the children their pre-school lessons.

'Next year the school bus will fetch Dimples every morning with all the pupils from round-about properties and return her in the afternoons,' she explained. 'It's compulsory. The schools have to be fully attended to keep going.'

So Rob and I often found ourselves at the swimming pool in the middle of the morning, lounging on the grass in the shade of a big palm. I learned that it was his ambition to dedicate his life to working among the Australian aboriginals, to build up their health and their standard of living.

'That's why I want to work in South Africa for a while,' he said. 'In Lesotho first, and then in some of your great multiracial hospitals. Our countries can learn from each other.'

'Kobie's learning a lot here at Sun Downs. He's absorbed in the place.'

We'd been in for a swim and my long hair clung to my shoulders. No point in drying it. We'd be in the water again any moment.

'Are you a good farmer's wife?' Rob asked with a smile. 'My sister's always so restless.'

'I love Springbok Spruit. I've known it most of my life. Kobie and his sister, Rita, and I were raised together. I like the peace and quiet of the country. Rita doesn't – except for short periods. She's studying drama.'

'So it's the stage for her?'

'The stage, the screen, T.V. – show business. She's quite a beauty.'

'Your type?'

I laughed. 'Goodness, no! A buttercup blonde, eyes like Kobie's – very bright blue. A lovely figure.'

'I like them small and dark.'

'Wait till you see Rita – maybe when you stay with us on your way to or from Lesotho.'

'One of these days . . . Has Springbok Spruit been in your family long?'

'Kobie's the third generation. Our son will be the fourth.'

'Your son!' He made a quick unconscious gesture of negation. 'Jo, you're not —'

I laughed. 'But yes – only a few weeks, but definitely yes. We just have to keep our fingers crossed for a boy.'

He wasn't wearing dark glasses. He seldom did, even in that brilliant Australian sunshine. He was staring at me with an expression of shock.

The laughter died from my lips.

'Rob – what is it?'

He said slowly: 'You had a baby. She died in infancy. Kobie told me.'

I nodded. I could speak about it now.

'I felt it was my fault in a way. If she made some little sound in the night, it didn't wake me.'

'After that baby's birth you had a hearing problem?' His eyes were grave and compassionate.

'Not much. A bit at times.'

79

We were both silent, but that was when I really began to understand what was happening to me.

A cloud obscured the sun. It seemed to move lower and advance upon me. The air, with its warm scent of frangipani, trembled and darkened. I was back in the Karoo, on the road to Springbok Spruit with Kobie and Rita, and Mr Van der Walt at the wheel of his car. We were children again. Crops were ripening and the grazing was good.

'Oh, God! Locusts! Close the windows, children!'

The cloud was quite dark now, flying towards us. Mr Van der Walt stopped the car while the swarm engulfed us, going its way regardless.

We heard the machine-gun spatter of the giant grasshoppers beating upon the radiator, the windscreen, windows and bonnet, hundreds of them, dead and broken as they struck the car. When the swarm had passed we got out and brushed off the crawling dismembered survivors. We were children of the veld. We knew that not one blade of grass or ear of grain would be left standing after their passage. Every green thing would be devoured.

So now, all these years later, another sinister destructive cloud advanced upon me – the problem I had so far resolutely refused to face. Clues, long disregarded, hammered at my consciousness like the locusts had beaten their tattoo of death on our car. Lessons unheard, winds and tides muffled, birds and cicadas silent, voices mumbling, sounds impossible to distinguish, Kobie's impatient leap across a room to turn down the radio I'd put on full blast, furtive glances of dismay at foolish answers to imperfectly heard questions, a baby's icy body freezing the blood in my veins and the milk in my breasts, Gran leaning on her stick against the winter wind on Muizenberg beach, pale and dizzy. 'It's not only old people who are hard of hearing, Jo-Jo. In certain cases childbirth increases the tendency. That's what happened to me.'

And to me. And it would happen even more so now. Was that the price of a son for Kobie and me and Springbok Spruit? A silent world for me.

The dark cloud was murkier. It was red, then inky black. Cold sweat was pouring off my forehead. Rob's fingers were on my pulse.

When I opened my eyes I had been lifted on to a chaise-longue and Rob was holding a glass of iced water to my lips.

'Are you all right now, Jo?'

I tried to smile. 'A touch of sun,' I said. 'Sorry. I just blacked right out.'

I rested in our cool air-conditioned bedroom all that afternoon, burning and chilled by turns with what Jennie and Kobie called 'sun fever'. But I knew it was more than that.

I'd faced my problem at last. Our child to come was no accident. He was wanted and welcome. But he would surely exact the cost of his growing life. Rob's unguarded look of dismay had told me that.

The chills that shook me that afternoon in the quiet darkened room were not fever.

They were shock.

PART TWO

Jo, Rob and Rita

9

THE THINGS YOU ARE AFRAID TO FACE YOU PUT OFF.
You try to ignore them.

Soon after our return to Springbok Spruit Kobie had to
go to his annual military camp. Before that he and Jan Bosman, the manager, were very busy. Kobie had learnt a great
deal from Jack Burton and was determined to apply many
new innovations on our own farm. Ma was keenly interested,
and somehow my personal problem was shelved. Or nearly.
The evening before Kobie left for camp, he brought the
subject up briefly.

'When I come back, Jo-Jo, we'll arrange to consult a
specialist about your hearing.'

We sat near the big landscape window of our living-room.
Far away the lavender Sneeuberg range broke the line
of the horizon, near at hand the willow-fringed dam reflected the spectacular gold and ruby of the sunset. I could
no longer hear the lowing of the cattle as they went to
drink.

Kobie was next to me on the couch, his arm about my
shoulders, our sundowners on the small stinkwood sofa-
table.

'Yes,' I said. 'When you come back.'

He gave me a squeeze and brushed his cheek against my hair.

'We'll find the answer, little one. Never fear.'

I thought of Gran, who had failed to find the answer, even in surgery, and shivered, drawing closer to Kobie's warmth. Somehow, he and I must keep the normal lines of communication open between us. Yet every day they seemed more scrambled. Wars could be lost by the breakdown of communications. What might happen to our marriage under the attack of this creeping invisible enemy?

Next morning Kobie left in the Land-Rover.

Ma and I watched the cloud of red dust cross the empty veld and disappear as the last fence gate was opened and closed and he turned south on to the tarmac of the National Road.

Christabel, my living-in help, the daughter of one of our coloured farm labourers, brought us eleven o'clock coffee on to the stoep. She had made feather-light scones, hot and buttery, and she wore a new pink *doek* like a turban on her frizzy hair out of respect for *die ounooi* who was much loved and revered.

'Your roses are still in bloom – quite lovely.' Ma looked at our garden with pleasure. 'You've made this place of yours so pretty – inside and out.'

The day was glorious as only a sunny autumn day can be, with its memory of summer and nip of winter, and the gold of leaf and veld grass. The air smelt of smoke and the distance was smoky blue. Ma bit into a scone with approval.

'You look wonderful, Jo.' Her shrewd glance appraised

my clear eyes and glowing skin. 'You take your pregnancies well.'

'In some ways, yes. I feel fine.'

'Why that note of doubt?'

'Listen, Ma. Our home is a quiet place – a good place for thinking-out problems.'

She smiled. 'What are your problems, my child? Tell me. Surely not your coming baby.'

'It's possible.' Suddenly I felt a great need to confide in her. With her Junoesque figure, her serene smile and crown of red-gold hair, she was an immensely reassuring personality. 'You remember my grandmother?'

She looked puzzled. 'Mrs Browning. Of course I do. She stayed with your parents at the time of your wedding.'

'You remember also that she was very deaf.'

Ma nodded. She sipped her coffee thoughtfully. 'People of her age often are, Jo.'

'So are people of my age. It can begin with puberty, and pregnancy makes it worse. That's how it was with my grandmother – how it *is* with me! I was beginning to have a hearing problem in my last years at school. That's why I did so badly. Nobody spotted it. Even I didn't realize what had hit me. It got worse after Mary Margerita was born. You noticed it then, didn't you? Please be honest with me . . . You see, we have to face this . . . Kobie and I.'

I saw her catch her breath and knew that the tension building up in me was being transmitted to her.

'You turned the radio up rather high,' she said at last. 'We had to speak a bit louder to get through to you —'

'You're doing that now – speaking louder than you would to Kobie? All right, you needn't answer. I know. It's getting worse, isn't it? *Isn't it?*'

My black spaniel, Darkie, sat up beside her, hoping for a scone. Her hand caressed his head.

'I'm a young woman,' I cried, 'but in a party I'm a dead loss. In Australia Kobie often got fed up with me. He blamed me for not concentrating – not paying attention. Once he said "Have you forgotten how to enjoy yourself?" He said that! I've begun to dread parties. What'll happen to Kobie and me? He likes a crowd, he's cheerful and full of fun. I'm frightened, Ma. After this baby is born it could be even worse . . .' I buried my face in my hands.

She reacted in her characteristically sensible way. She got up and rang the bell. She told Christabel to take the tray away. She remembered to compliment her on the scones. All this gave me time to get a hold on myself. Voicing my fears had given them a terrible destructive power. I was choked with them.

'Come on, Jo,' she said. 'Let's get down to brass tacks. I suggest you go and stay with your parents now – while Kobie's away in camp. Make an immediate appointment with Dr Du Toit and get his advice. He's experienced and wise. He knows your family history —'

'I won't have surgery. Look what happened to Gran! She can never swim, she's often giddy. She needs a hearing-aid —'

'Perhaps you need a hearing-aid too, my child.'

'Oh, no! I'd feel a freak – like an old woman.'

'Nonsense! With your lovely hair, and the way you wear

it – long, hanging over your shoulders – not a soul would ever know if you had some tiny attachment behind your ear. As you say – you're young. You must get the best out of life. You're very good to look at, you have the use of your limbs, you ride, dance, surf, play games, make love. You can *see*. To be crippled, to be blind – there's tragedy. To be hard of hearing – well, that's bad luck, it may be quite a problem, but it's no tragedy.'

I looked into her blue eyes, so like Kobie's, and saw there the exasperation I had seen in his when he had felt I wasn't 'trying hard enough'. She too was blaming me for 'not making an effort'.

'Tragedy? What does that mean? Is a marriage under strain no tragedy?'

'Nobody's talking about a marriage under strain.'

'I am. There were moments in Perth when I knew Kobie was criticizing me for not being able to join in. He couldn't seem to understand —'

'Jo!' she cut in. 'I'm putting my mind to this problem – trying to give you sensible advice. Yet, at the very mention of a hearing-aid, you fly up —'

'I've seen my gran struggling with hers.'

'Perhaps your grandmother didn't persevere enough —'

'So it's her fault!'

'You're being unreasonable. You came out with your real objection the moment I uttered the word hearing-aid. You said you'd . . . feel a freak. You don't feel a freak when you wear your sunglasses. But a tiny contrivance in your ear? *No!*' Her voice – raised, no doubt – was astringent. 'This is

89

no case for false vanity and self pity – I'm being frank, you see – it's a case for finding the best solution to quite a common problem.'

I rose, the blood hot in my cheeks, tears of rage and frustration brightening my eyes but not spilling over. For the first time in my life I felt that Kobie's mother was letting me down.

'False vanity and self pity! So that's what you boil it down to? Ma, you talk like a predikant. In a minute you'll tell me to kneel down and pray for humility and courage!'

She stood up and put her hands on my trembling shoulders, looking down at me from her greater height, the quick unconscious spark of impatience fading from her glance as fast as it had come. Her expression was grave, tinged with disappointment. Somehow we had failed each other. We were both aware of it.

'You could do worse, my child,' she said, gently. 'You could do worse than kneel down and pray.'

A couple of days later I did as my mother-in-law had suggested and went to stay with Daddy and Mummy in Verfontein.

Our little town was packed with country visitors who had come to the Trade Fair. I was one of them. But when Mummy suggested we go together I made excuses. I went alone.

The fair-ground was crowded and taped music made a constant din. Old schoolfriends greeted me but I shook them off, promising to give them a ring next day.

But Mrs Geldenhuys wasn't so easily put off. She was a local character, crippled with arthritis. Her coloured maid, nearly as ancient as her mistress, pushed her wheelchair everywhere. Mrs Geldenhuys' darting venerable eyes missed nothing, either at the Zebra Shopping Centre or now at the Fair.

'Jo!' she cried when she spotted me. 'Why don't you come to town more often, you naughty girl? What are you here for?' She didn't wait for an answer. 'I'm deaf as a post these days and there's a fellow here testing people for hearing-aids. Over there in that booth —'

'I'm going that way. I'll walk with you.'

In fact, I was at the Fair for the same purpose as Mrs Geldenhuys. She went into the booth first and emerged beaming.

'He's coming to my house tomorrow to fit me for one of those gadgets. You're only a youngster, you wouldn't know about such things.'

Wouldn't I though? I tried to laugh as I stood and watched her being wheeled away. Then I took my turn.

The young man in charge was bright and breezy. He put head-phones over my ears and sat me down.

'I have a hearing problem,' I said, 'and I want to know just how bad it really is. For instance, I know it's nothing like as bad as old Mrs Geldenhuys who's just been here in her wheelchair. But maybe I do need an aid.'

When he'd done his testing, he stood looking at me with the most extraordinary mixture of dismay and triumph. I still wore the amplifying ear-phones.

'I hate to tell you,' he said, 'but you're far worse than old Mrs Geldenhuys. Now don't take on, Mrs Van der Walt! Your sort of deafness is fine for our merchandise. No trouble at all to fix you up. Give me your address and I'll be along to see you tomorrow.'

He was as good as his word. He fitted me with a tiny contraption like a bubble. He showed me how to use it and supplied me with the electric cells I'd need. There was an agent in the Zebra Shopping Centre who'd order new ones when necessary.

Dr Du Toit examined my ears and was all in favour of the aid. He explained that my type of deafness was fairly prevalent among women – especially white women. The Bantu didn't suffer from it. There was surgery, but he didn't advise it yet. New methods were being developed. It might be wise to limit my family. Pregnancies could aggravate the condition. A bit late to tell me that!

The little contraption was a wonderful help. But when I put it on my bedside table that night and turned off the reading lamp, I lay wide-eyed in the silent dark. Pillow-talk, a baby's whimper, a telephone ringing, the hoot of an owl, the whisper of the wind, a dog barking, a car passing down Main Street . . . none of these would ever disturb my sleep again. I was 'far worse than old Mrs Geldenhuys'. I was twenty but I felt as old as time.

❧ 10 ❧

BY THE TIME KOBIE RETURNED FROM CAMP I HAD learned to use my new hearing-aid intelligently.

He was incredulous and relieved. He took my face between his hard farmer's hands with great gentleness and tilted it up so that my hair fell away from my ears. He touched the tiny aid.

'This little bubble behind your ear – why, liefie, it's magic! And not a soul could notice it. You're wonderful – going to that trade fair all alone and trying it out, and then getting Dr Du Toit's approval.'

It seemed then that our problem was solved.

Gerrit Joseph van der Walt was born in Verfontein Hospital on a stormy September morning. Like his sister, he was a spring lamb.

When he was ten days' old Kobie fetched us home. I insisted that the baby should sleep in our bedroom. For just one moment Kobie fought my decision.

'Must we do this? Can't we have him in the dressing-room?'

'You know why we must,' I said.

He looked straight into my eyes and saw the reason there. He put his arms round me without a word and held me very

93

close. You don't argue with the ghost of a dead baby. What had happened to Mary Margerita must never happen to Gert.

For a while after Gert's birth we were very happy.

The baby heir to Springbok Spruit was sturdy, healthy and contented, with a fluff of honey-coloured curls and the clear blue Van der Walt eyes. Kobie and Ma were as mad about him as I was.

The little 'bubble' was my stand-by but I seldom bothered to wear it on the farm. Why should I? Kobie and Ma always spoke up to me. That this might be tiresome for them seldom occurred to me. Christabel had a voice like a police whistle, and for the rest our life was peaceful. When friends came over for the weekend or for the day I wore it, though it was always rather disappointing in a crowd. Distinguishing voices and sounds was difficult, although they were amplified. I began to jib at inviting weekend houseparties and, when Kobie insisted, I was more and more inclined to withdraw. I found excuses to dodge the cheerful sessions at the pool or round the embers at the outdoor barbecues – the *braais* Kobie enjoyed so much.

'You're so unsociable these days, liefie,' Kobie reproached me once. 'You used to be such fun – a lovely dancing girl full of mischief and laughter and now you're turning into a sort of recluse!'

When Gert was a few months' old and we went to stay with Gran for our summer holiday it was the same. I was increasingly unsociable.

One day we took our baby to Stellenbosch to introduce

him to Kobie's Erasmus relations. In the afternoon friends of Kobie's schooldays brought their young wives in to tea – a real Afrikaner spread with everybody hearty and appreciative. There were other babies and little children and old folk and by the time we were in the car and driving back to Muizenberg I was exhausted. Gert slept on my lap, I took the little bubble out of my ear and settled down to relax.

'Put that thing back,' demanded Kobie. 'I want to talk to you, Jo.'

I obeyed him reluctantly.

'Did you have to make it so clear to my folk that they bored you?' He looked hurt and annoyed.

I knew I must have appeared quiet. I just hadn't been able to keep pace with disjointed conversations conducted in a mixture of Afrikaans and English.

'I'm sorry if I disappointed the Professor and Mrs Erasmus – and your cousins and friends,' I said, cold and unrepentant.

'Everybody tried to make you feel at home but you just wouldn't play.'

'Half the time I didn't know who was talking or what about – or even which language was being used. It was Bedlam!'

'So that's your opinion of my people's hospitality —'

'Oh, shut up, Kobie!'

'You don't try —'

'I don't *concentrate*. It's all my fault.' I turned on him like a viper. 'You're the patient saint. Leave me in peace – just let me alone!'

'That's what Rita tells me to do – leave you to go into

95

your own private world where you feel safe and don't have to make any effort. A world away from the rest of us.'

I took the bubble from my ear and put it ostentatiously in my bag. I didn't bother to answer. For all Kobie knew, I might not have heard him. I saw him shrug his shoulders and wrinkle his eyes against the low sun. His firm blunt profile was set and stubborn. I closed my eyes and deliberately detached myself from the situation. Rita was dead right. I *could* go into a private world almost at will.

I shut my eyes to Kobie's irritation, to the growing rift between us, to the signpost that warned me I was taking a lonely defeatist turning. I had reached the point I think of now as the U-turn.

The U-turn? The signpost at that crucial bend in the road has two arms. One says Out-to-the-World and the other says Retreat-into-Self. Perhaps, when you are old and tired, there is nothing to fear in the long journey back – only a certain solitary restfulness with memories as milestones. No challenge of the unknown. But, when you're young, it's a sad, perilous journey leading away from the turmoil and stress and joy of active life back into the dark recess of self.

My grandmother had made it, lighting the gloom of her peaceful inner solitude with a student's interests. Reading, writing, embroidering beautifully, painting badly, observing the noisy summer scene on the crowded beaches that were, to her, so silent. When I came into her life as a very young teenager she was forced into a sort of emergence and I believe she enjoyed it. But by then she had established her retreat and I had quickly learned to respect it. She was old and alone and entitled to it.

Now, because she was wise and experienced too, and better able to understand my problem than anyone else, she decided to take me to task.

'Jo-Jo,' she said one day when Kobie was out playing golf with a friend, 'you're dodging life more than you ought. You're giving too much time to Gert and not enough to Kobie. Maria and I are quite capable of taking care of Gert.'

'Gert's no trouble to me, Gran.'

'And Kobie is?'

'He likes a crowd. He draws people round him. He doesn't need me all the time.'

'You have a young attractive husband. He's in love with you. Don't take your blessings for granted. Make great efforts to hold on to them.'

'Make more effort . . . How often I hear that!'

'People like you and I have to make special efforts. We must! It's our duty. We have to learn to read lips and faces, and we have to do a lot of guessing – and hope we guess right.' She laughed. 'Mind you, people overlook it if we don't! You're very young and very pretty, you can't opt out – and use Gert for an excuse, as you're doing more and more, Jo.'

I told myself she was talking so much because it was easier than listening, but, in fact, I knew she was really trying to help me. I said defensively:

'We don't squabble on the farm – when we're more or

less alone together. I love Springbok Spruit, Gran. It's a . . . sort of haven as well as a home.'

'So long as it doesn't become a hide-out,' she said brusquely. 'Now, go dancing with that inexhaustible husband of yours tonight and we'll put Gert's cot in my room as we always do when you're out.'

Springbok Spruit was indeed becoming a hide-out for me. I had Kobie, my baby son and Ma for company always close at hand, and Mrs Bosman, the manager's wife and her family over the hill, and neighbours within a radius of fifty kilometres and Verfontein not much farther away. I was happy to be home again.

The winter was as bright and bracing as ever – colder than usual, with the snow drifts deep on the mountains, and even the koppies topped with glittering white. The tall candelabra of the aloes blazed in the bush, but it was a bad year for the farmers. The summer rains had failed and violent electric storms and winter hail had destroyed many of the sheep. Our own boreholes were good and proof against drought but farmers in dryer areas suffered heavy losses.

Kobie took the plight of the stricken zones deeply to heart. From childhood he had been taught by his father that agriculture – not gold – was the true backbone of South Africa and that farmers must therefore stand together and help each other. It was part of his creed that Springbok Spruit, well watered and well established through the unremitting efforts of generations of enterprising Van der Walts, must aim to be a go-ahead, co-operative example in our wool-producing part of the Karoo.

During that cruel summer when the *vleis* – wide shallow lakes beloved of the birds – turned from sheets of shining water to desolate mud wastes, dried and cracked by the relentless sun, Kobie was able, at a sacrifice, to offer grazing to less fortunate farmers' sheep for as long as we could help support them. Ma and tough Jannie Bosman backed him up and flocks from the thirstland trekked on to our property to be saved by our underground water. So I watched my young husband, who, but for his father's sudden violent death, would still have been a carefree student at Cape Town University, beginning to shoulder the burdens of our great mountainous plateau, where drought, flood, hail and pests struck with equal ferocity when all seemed to be going well.

That winter we heard from Rob Stirling in Australia.

He was planning to work as a surgical registrar at Groote Schuur Hospital in the following year. Meanwhile he hoped to join the South African flying doctor in Lesotho and study health conditions in other emergent African states. However, his first stop would be Cape Town to collect medical supplies for Lesotho and also to settle the matter of his appointment at Groote Schuur.

Kobie wrote and gave him various introductions to friends at the Cape, and, of course, to Rita who was in her final year at varsity and already making quite a name for herself in theatrical productions connected with the university. 'Come and see us when you can,' he wrote. 'Rita usually spends her spring vacation here and if you come with her you'll be right on your way to Lesotho.'

So they came together – Rob and Rita – soon after Gert's first birthday. Rob drove her over the dramatic Cape passes to the high plateau of the Karoo in his big station-wagon packed with supplies and valuable equipment for the hospital at Maseru, the capital of the little independent mountain kingdom of Lesotho in the heart of the Republic.

Rob stayed with Ma and Rita in the homestead. I had forgotten – or perhaps I had tried not to remember – how attractive he was to me. The long supple limbs, the thick black hair, the lively hazel eyes that looked at you so straight and could be suddenly serious or alight with humour. The deep flexible voice that evoked exciting responsive vibrations in my nerves.

'What d'you think of our Australian?' I asked Rita when we were alone for a few moments on the evening of their arrival.

She had strolled down to our house with me before going back to the homestead to bath and change for dinner.

There was dust on her thick lashes and her shoulder length hair was tangled and amber-gold in the setting sun. She shot me a laughing inquisitive glance.

'You really want to know, don't you?'

I nodded, feeling myself colour under that quick perceptive scrutiny.

'I'll tell you then. I reckon your Australian plays hard to get . . . no, *plays* is the wrong word . . . Rob Stirling *is* hard to get.' She paused and now her eyes were clouded, almost grey as they met mine. 'You tell me why!'

I looked at the fine-featured face and slim seductive figure of my sister-in-law. Surely no man would be hard for her to get? Her experience was timeless. Rita had been all woman from the day the hazy veils of babyhood had faded from her eyes, just as a kitten is all cat the moment its infantile blindness has passed.

'Well?' she probed.

'It's hard for any one person to . . . get . . . Rob. He belongs to all the people who need him – the sick and the poor —'

'Come off it, Jo!' Her sudden laugh was brittle and the briefly clouded gaze was sharp with cynicism. 'He may be a bit of an idealist, but he's also a man – one hundred per cent male.'

'There's your challenge then.'

'It's a long drive from the Cape to the Karoo.' She threw me an odd smile. 'Rob spent a good deal of it asking questions about you.'

'You could certainly answer them. No one better.'

'We've been brought up like sisters – yet sometimes I wonder . . .'

'What do you wonder?'

'If we really know each other through and through. So much of life is acting, playing a part.'

'For you, yes. My life is here. Without an audience there's not much point in playing a part.'

She smiled. 'You have an audience now. A fascinated audience. For the next two weeks. Choose your mask, little

Jo-Jo. Farmer's contented wife, young mother, devoted daughter-in-law . . . or restless girl caught in a too early marriage —'

'You won't ever make that mistake, will you, Rita?'

'There's no room for a husband and a baby in my life at present. One day, yes. Not yet. But a lover —'

'Who is he?'

'Just now there's a vacuum.'

'Nature abhors —'

She flung a tanned bare arm across my shoulders.

'Exactly! And who am I to go against nature? See you and Kobie later. I hope Ma has prepared a good dinner. Rob and I are a pair of hungry wolves.'

I watched her saunter up the rise, soft fair hair blowing about her well-poised head. Rob came down the homestead path to meet her. The sky flamed above them, the veld grass was washed with rose. The far ranges were rosy too. They walked in beauty side by side.

🎕 11 🎕

THERE WAS MAGIC IN THE AIR THAT SPRING WHEN
Rob came to us for the first time. Perhaps it was the joyous-
ness of the season – or it could have been the frank admiration
in his eyes – that made me conscious once more of my own
vibrant youth. For him I came out of my shell and made all
the efforts that Kobie could have wished – though my husband greeted them with less delight and enthusiasm than I
might have anticipated!

The Karoo, ever resilient, matched my mood. It glowed
and bloomed after the drought was broken by an unpredict-
able out-of-season rainfall soaking the veld and filling the
vleis. A host of many coloured wild flowers burst out of the
moist earth to greet the sun – jewel-bright carpets of amethyst; topaz and ruby *vygies;* quivering orange and yellow
Namaqualand daisies; blue *babianas,* miniature irises, chin-
cherinchees, and, on the koppies, clove-scented clusters of
pinks and tufts of heather. The air was laden with the
fragrance of aromatic bush and alive with flocks of little
darting birds and the swoop and twitter of the first swallows
from far northern lands. Waterfowl flirted on the shining
coppery dams, and baby animals frolicked beside their
mothers – foals, lambs, fawns, tiny meerkats!

It was a busy time for Kobie and Jannie Bosman and the shearers in the sheds, so Rita and I took care of Rob. He was entranced when he saw a team of sixteen oxen ploughing on the skyline – a frieze of the past long forgotten in his own highly mechanized country. We reined in our ponies to let him watch the leisurely process.

'The way that little yellow-brown man talks to his oxen – all clicks – and the crack of his long whip! What sort of native is he? He's not like your Cape coloured, or an American Negro, or even those fine-looking Bantu I saw around Cape Town. He's got a wedge-shaped face and a remarkably protuberant posterior.'

'He comes from Namaqualand,' I said. 'He's a descendant of the Bushmen who once inhabited this plain till they were driven into the mountains by the Hottentots and stronger tribes.'

'You'll still see Bushmen in the Kalahari and South West Africa,' put in Rita. 'They're desert hunters. There are mountain caves round here with Bushmen paintings on the walls. All hunting scenes, of course.'

'I'd like to see one of those caves,' Rob said.

'We can go on Sunday when Kobie's free. Take a picnic. Ma, Gert, all of us,' I suggested eagerly.

Rita smiled, surprised at my animation. Her expression told me more clearly than words how dull I must have become. When we put the plan to Ma, she decided that the day would be too long for Gert. So she took charge of her grandson while the four of us went in Kobie's car.

We left it in the foothills of the Sneeuberg and climbed

high up the mountainside to a big overhanging rock cave, its sandstone walls adorned with paintings of animals and thin naked hunters in lively movement. At first it was difficult to distinguish the ochre-coloured beasts and figures, but as our eyes grew accustomed to the gloom we discovered more and more detail.

'How old are these paintings?' Rob asked.

'Nobody knows for certain,' said Kobie. 'Say five centuries, give or take a hundred years. There are caves like this in many of our mountains and, from the pictures, we know what animals roamed the plains and hills in the days before the hunter with the gun.'

'Some of the pictures are ceremonial.' Rita traced a design of men with bows and arrows, wearing masks of animals. 'All their ritual was to do with wild animals. In fact, the early Boers in South Africa regarded Bushmen as half animal – a sort of missing link.'

'Is the race extinct in the Karoo?' asked Rob.

'Nearly,' said Kobie. 'But you can find some of their descendants about. Like the ox-herd who intrigued you so much. They are unique survivals from way back in the Stone Age. They can divine water where no one else can, they know every plant and its properties; every poison, from the tiny wild iris to the cobra; they can weave spells; and, when it comes to hunting, they have extra-sensory perception to the last degree. They literally feel the presence of game – its moods and dangers – in their own skin and bones.'

He went to the mouth of the cave and looked down over the bush.

'What a lookout post!'

Rob joined him. 'It's wonderful. I wonder how their skin and bones reacted when they saw the first trek-wagons and the domestic flocks and herds of white men – to say nothing of the white men themselves.'

'My God, I hate to think! Poor little beggars, they must have had some pretty fearful sensations when that happened.'

'With good reason. Think of our own aboriginals at home, or the Incas and Aztecs and Red Indians – just to quote a few. Whether they greeted the Pale Faces as Gods or invaders they were in for the big take-over. Their way of life was doomed —'

'It didn't happen to the yellow races,' remarked Rita.

Rob's thin face in the deep shade of the overhanging cliff was thoughtful.

'Not in the Far East – not even after World War Two. The yellow races are another proposition, the product of civilizations much older than our own. Japan needs living space – elbow room for her vast population; minerals. She has a slant eye on my country. And China has already infil-trated Central Africa from east to west with strong tentacles moving south down your continent. Who can stop her? Your Gert will see some interesting changes in the next fifty years – just as the last watchers from this ritual cave saw the birth of a new era.'

Kobie put his arm round me as if to still a shudder of apprehension that brought the goosepimples out on my skin.

The atavistic spirit of the last cave artists seemed to stir

about us with faint mockery, as if they sensed that the ultimate fate of Africa was man hunting man to the death.

'What are you so afraid of, liefie?' Kobie's chin nuzzled
gently against my hair.

I pointed to the leaping ochre figures on the cave wall,
armed with their poisoned arrows.

'Their era was the Struggle for Survival,' I said. 'Gert's
will be the Era of Vengeance.'

I was quiet and absorbed with my thoughts as we drove
home through the veld already steeped in the drama of the
Karoo sunset. I was intensely aware of the four of us – all so
unalike – and of the destiny that drew us together. Rob, the
stranger from a far continent, dedicated to the alleviation of
suffering, especially the suffering of the ignorant and under-
privileged; Rita, self-willed, ambitious, talented and lovely;
Kobie with his roots deep in the land he loved, a man of
strong passions, kind, impulsive and undisciplined; and me,
his 'little bird' – the spirit of our old fig tree. Rita had said
once that I had the quality of a dryad – elusive, with a
temperament of dappled light and shade. But then Rita had
lyrical fits, depending upon the play in which she was performing. She could be poetic or crudely realistic. Of the four
of us, I thought, the one I knew least was probably myself.

Suddenly Kobie stopped the car so that we could watch a
herd of springbok bounding across the veld.

Rob was enthralled. 'Our 'roos are impressive, but there's
nothing to touch the sheer vital beauty of an antelope. I've
heard of springbok migrations. Have you ever seen one?'

Kobie shook his head. 'The last great migration was before we were born, but our pa saw one when he was a boy. The whole veld was alive with leaping buck. They grazed it bare. They were shot by farmers and skinned by blacks, but still they came, wave after wave, leaving barren lands and dead animals in their wake.'

'Like the lemmings – just going on till they fall over the cliff and into the sea—an instinctive break on our over-population.'

Kobie considered. 'I think perhaps not quite the same – not a completely mindless migration to destruction. More likely they were seeking new feeding grounds —'

'Like birds,' I suggested.

He shrugged. 'Could be. It's instinct anyway.'

'Curious thing, instinct,' said Rob. 'In a mob instinct is irresistible. Some leader sparks it off and the mob goes along with it regardless. But, even in the individual, instinct makes an end of reason.'

'Instinct can be more sensible than reason,' said Kobie.

My gaze rested on my husband's profile as he stared intently after the vanishing herd. He had filled out since the teenage days when we had first acknowledged our love for each other. His throat and shoulders were powerful, he had the tanned tireless look of a man born to the active hardy life of a true farmer. Rita, who so often put her finger pain-fully on the spot, had once said of her brother: 'Kobie's so earthy it's a wonder his nails are ever clean! But then, earthy or not, he doesn't have to do his own dirty work. He calls a man with a brown face to do it for him. That's our way of life.' By instinct Kobie was a hunter – a man descended from pioneers who had killed game not for sport but to provide their dependants with food. By training he was a conservator of wild life and the soil. Instinct and reason were often at variance in his disposition. He's a basic human being, I thought. He'd fight to the death against any threat to his country or his home and family. In the last extremity he'd act by instinct rather than reason.

And I? What would I do? In the last extremity there might be no time for reason to operate. Instinct would have to be the guide.

❦ 12 ❦

THAT VISIT OF ROB'S WAS ALARMINGLY UNSETTLING for me.

I must have gone far into my own private retreat before he'd arrived – much further than I'd realized. Now I longed most intensely to be back with the world, wherever I might find it. We went dancing one Saturday night in Verfontein and afterwards, back home in our bedroom, Kobie made a scene.

'Did you have to dance with Rob like that?'

'Like what?'

'As if you were . . . sort of welded together.'

His own type of dancing was athletic and exuberant, the two partners each doing their own thing and only coming together part of the time.

'Everybody dances differently.'

'You can see Rita's keen for Rob. Why butt in?'

I did the thing that I knew infuriated him. Switched him off. It was simple. I just gave him a certain look and took the bubble out of my ear. I saw the flash of his eyes and the set of his jaw, and later, when he made love to me, it was all there – the silent storm of possessive jealousy, the fire of angry youth, the excitement that added a sort of savage gusto to our moments of love–hate.

Afterwards, when we were at peace, he held me close against him with my head in the crook of his shoulder. I knew then that he needed me and was afraid of Rob.

The wind blew icily across the veld the day Rob and Rita left us. He drove her to Bloemfontein where they were to spend the night. Next day he'd see her off to the Cape by air and then he'd continue on his way into the mountains of Lesotho.

That evening I was restless and shivery.

'These cold snaps between spring and summer are often the sharpest,' said Ma. 'There might even be another snow-fall on the Sneeuberg.' She had a fire crackling in the sitting-room.

When we were alone, I said to Kobie: 'What'll they do tonight? Dance, I suppose. It's a Saturday.'

'Sure.' He was watching me as he added: 'That welded way Rob has of dancing – if he likes his partner.'

'Do you suppose . . .?'

He laughed.

'They're young and vigorous. Wouldn't you in her place?'

'Curious that you don't seem to mind how permissive your sister is!'

'I believe she's discriminating. Not promiscuous.'

'Very discriminating. She told me once that she was only interested in lovers who could advance her stage career.'

'And what if she falls in love with somebody not connected with the stage?'

What indeed?

'She won't. She knows where she's going.'

'Do any of us?'

I knew then that he wanted Rita and Rob to be lovers. That way he reckoned I'd be safe.

Rita wanted it too. For the simple reason that, for the first time, she was swept off her feet. In love.

It started that night in Bloemfontein. It was resumed early in the following year when Rob left his short survey of backward African states and took up his post as a surgical registrar at Groote Schuur.

By the time we got to the Cape at the end of February for our annual holiday at the sea with Gran the relationship was established.

'It was love at first sight,' said Kobie, as he and I sat on the beach in the sun watching Gert build sandcastles that were soon demolished by the incoming tide.

'There's no such thing.'

'Of course there is! What about you and me?'

'Oh, Kobie, you are funny! I think you really believe that.'

'Well, don't you?' His blue eyes laughed into mine, but they were disarmingly naïve – as trusting as Gert's.

'Of course not. I resented you to madness, and all you wanted was to get a solid footing in *my* tree.'

'The best climbing tree in Africa,' he admitted with a grin. 'Maybe I delude myself.'

'As for Rob and Rita. She saw him and she said to herself "That's for me!" and that – in time – was bound to be the end of Rob. If a woman as lovely and intelligent and determined as your sister wants a man he hasn't a hope.'

'Would you say he's lucky?'

'I'd say they're both lucky. He's crazy about his work and she's crazy about her career. Marriage doesn't come into it. They have what's called a meaningful relationship.'

'I'd rather see my sister enter into a meaningful marriage.'

'Relationships are flexible these days. If they work out well they could end in marriage. If not they're written off as experience.'

'Thank God we have a son! I'd go berserk if a daughter of ours got involved in a . . . flexible relationship. She'd probably find herself ditched at the end of it.'

'Maybe we'll have a daughter one of these days.'

He turned to me, his face shocked.

'Not if I can help it! Remember what the doctor said? For God's sake, liefie, aren't you deaf enough as it is?'

It was like a blow. I gasped. He could hurt me so much without even meaning to. He was so often the bull in my all-too-vulnerable china shop of self-confidence.

That was a bad year for our sheep farmers. Synthetics and a world economic depression had hit the wool trade and the brief pre-spring rains had only offered a respite from the drought that now held most of the Karoo in its grip.

Summer, autumn, winter and the following spring were dry as dead bones. We still had enough sweet grass on Springbok Spruit to sustain our own beasts and help our neighbours, but other areas had become dustbowls and sheep and cattle died of thirst before they could reach the abattoirs. The soil was as dry and wrinkled as an ancient face.

One day, towards the end of the year, when Kobie returned from Verfontein he brought the mail up to the homestead where Gert and I were with Ma. He was hot but smiling as he bounded up the stoep steps and into the cool sitting-room. When he'd greeted us and hugged his son, he flung the batch of letters on to the table.

'One of those is really interesting,' he said.

We'd been having tea and Ma poured him a cup, strong and sweet, the way he liked it.

'Tell us more,' she said.

'It's an invitation to attend an Agricultural World Conference in San Francisco next March. The emphasis is on soil and water conservation and increased productivity.'

I had to ask him to repeat what he had said. He made an impatient gesture towards the letters.

'Read it, Jo. It's on top.'

When I'd read the letter I handed it to Ma. As she took it I turned to Kobie.

'How long would you be away?'

'As you've seen, it involves a considerable tour. I'd say at least six weeks – if Ma and Jan Bosman will hold the fort.'

There was a pause as Ma finished reading the letter. She folded it and returned it to her son.

'This is important – for us and for the Karoo. Of course you must go. You're better situated to leave your farm than most farmers on the plain. Jan and I can keep things going here. We often have done before.'

She looked at me, her eyes commanding rather than questioning. 'Of course you'll go with Kobie, Jo. Your parents will love to have Gert. I'll be very busy here without Kobie. It wouldn't be quite so easy for me to take care of him.'

'Naturally.' Kobie had finished his tea and Gert was riding on his knee. 'This boy's no problem. He's good-natured and healthy and Jo's ma always says she wishes there was a child in the house again —'

'I know she'd want him,' I agreed. 'He'd be all right there.'

'Then why do you look so doubtful?'

'I have to think about this, Ma. I can't say right off whether I want to go or not. It sounds a very intensive tour . . . involving a lot of new places . . . and people —'

'Surely an exciting prospect?' she persisted.

Kobie stopped jogging Gert on his knee and stared at me as if he were trying to fathom the workings of my mind.

New places, new voices, foreigners, quick American wise-cracks, receptions . . . I was always at a loss in crowds, confused by quickly changing topics of conversation. Kobie'd be occupied all day, I'd be left to the lavish hospitality of the American wives. It was legendary, they'd be wonderful, but I'd be an embarrassment and a pest. With the lines of communication so seriously impaired, I'd be no asset to Kobie or anyone else.

'I must think it through,' I said doggedly.

When Ma opened her mouth to protest Kobie raised his hand and frowned at her.

'No, Ma, leave this to Jo. It's for her to decide what she wants to do.' He added gently: 'Jo has difficulties. This tour, with its social obligations for the wives, could put a great strain on her.'

Ma nodded, but her face was troubled and obstinate and I knew this wasn't the end of the matter as far as she was concerned.

She came down to see me the very next morning, sure of finding me back from my early morning ride on Chief. The dry heat seemed to crackle over the dehydrated veld and already the far mountains and the near koppies paddled in mirage, but many dams that had held real water had turned into a brown crazy paving of parched earth where the springbok came in vain to quench their thirst. A warm nervous Berg wind set the windmills clonking. I saw the tall figure stride purposefully down the dusty path through parchment pale grass. I went to meet her, my hair blowing about my face.

'You girls never wear hats. You'll have leather complexions at my age.'

Her little red parasol shaded her face and her coronet of bright hair. She could afford to talk. Her skin was still remarkably fresh and unlined for a woman in her forties.

I led her into the house. It was too hot to sit on the stoep.

'Tea or coffee, Ma?'

'Lemon-barley, if you have it.'

'Of course. Me too. It's a day for a cool drink.'

I got the jug of home-made lemon-barley from the fridge and two glasses. Gert was playing in his shady sandpit near the rose garden where the coloured gardener was spraying for black spot. I didn't call my son to welcome his *ouma* as I guessed she had something on her mind – and what it was.

She wasted no time.

'Well, Jo? Are you going with Kobie to America?'

'No, Ma. I'm not going. He'll be better on his own.'

'Have you told him that?'

'Not yet.'

'Then reconsider your decision.'

'I'm sorry. But, no.'

'You know I'm not one for interfering —'

'Anything but. You've seldom offered advice unasked.'

'I do it now – as I did when I advised you to build your own home. I do it because I don't like seeing you and Kobie drift apart. You're right for each other. You belong together.'

'Are we . . . drifting?'

Her gaze examined her strong firm hands – hands like her sons – as they lay in her lap.

'Sometimes I fear so.'

'Why?'

She looked up in that very direct way of hers that balked no issues.

'You're travelling a lonely road, Jo. All the time you seem to go deeper into some safe private world of your own – an inner world where Kobie can't follow you.'

I know now – though I didn't then – that my mother-in-law was more aware of the dangerous U-turn I had taken than I was myself. I hadn't seen the signpost along that 'lonely road'. She had.

'Safe private world' indeed! I was overcome anew by the familiar feeling of resentment at being held guilty for the thing that was not my fault. I wanted no 'inner world'. I longed achingly for the normal world of other people – to be able to communicate effortlessly in the serious, joking, complex, broken way of half-uttered thoughts that makes up ordinary human relationships. Ideas tossed easily back and forth and developed. Or confidences. Who'll shout a confidence at someone who may mishear and mangle it? Intimate secrets and allusions are whispered. Nobody ever whispered to me.

I rose, my cheeks burning.

'Kobie understands me very well, Ma. Only yesterday afternoon he said to you, "Leave this to Jo. It's for her to decide." I think you must let us do as we think best.'

She turned away from me as Gert ran in from his sandpit to demand lemonade and the attention of his *ouma*. She stooped to hug him and a bad moment was averted.

When Gert was in bed that night Kobie and I had our after-dinner coffee on the stoep. The wind had dropped and the summer evening was hot and calm with a myriad stars diamond-bright in the moonless purple sky. Here and there we could see the glimmer of egrets roosting in the willows like white flowers. I set Kobie's cup of strong black coffee beside him. He watched me add milk and sugar to mine. When I was lazily settled in the comfortable cane chair with a footrest, he said:

'This San Francisco conference, Jo – it's in March – three months from now. How do you feel about it?'

'How do you? Do you want very much to go?'

'Very much indeed. You haven't seen as much as I have of this whole area since the drought. It's heart-breaking! Good hard-working farmers ruined, leaving their land to seek work in the towns. They can't sell for love or money now. We can keep going at Springbok Spruit, but there are many who can't.'

He began to pace up and down, letting his coffee grow cold.

'The Americans have the answers to arid zones. They use their rivers and their underground water to the best advantage. There's so much I could learn over there. Crops that withstand dry seasons and pests, succulents animals can live on in semi-desert conditions – oh, there's so much I've read in agricultural magazines that I'd be able to study for myself on the spot. The world gets hungrier every year and we men of the land *must* help to feed it. We dare not go under! The Americans are tremendously aware of this.'

I took him as seriously as he took himself and his mission, but I smiled as I said:

'And when you come home you'll spread the productive gospel in the Karoo.'

He grinned. 'That's what I aim to do. Produce more food – and fewer children.'

The last words were sharp as a stiletto to me.

'You say that – about fewer children – because of me – to make me feel it doesn't matter that we must limit our family.'

'You're over sensitive, liefie.'

He drained his coffee and came and sat on my footrest. I tucked my bare feet up to give him room. He stroked them softly. 'You always kick off your sandals, don't you? No wonder. Such pretty feet – small and straight, like all of you. Jo-Jo, are you coming with me?'

'No, darling. I'm not.'

He was wearing crisp white shorts and a thin sports shirt open at the neck. His head was bent and the dim stoep light gilded his thick fair hair.

'I want you with me,' he said.

I leaned forward and took his hand.

'And I want to be with you – but things are getting worse for me. The bubble's all right when it's just you and me talking quietly together – like now, with everything so still – but it's no good any more in a crowd. And we'd be in crowds all the time. Strangers. You'd always be trying to draw me into conversations —'

'I'd help you —'

'You couldn't . . . much. I'd feel conspicuous – a drag on you. When you come back we'll consult that specialist in Johannesburg again. Find out how much worse I really am.'

'The one we went to six months ago? He said surgery was possible, but you wouldn't consider it.'

'Not after what happened to Gran. But maybe he could

suggest a stronger aid or something. Here – at Springbok Spruit – it doesn't seem to matter my being . . . deaf. It's almost restful —'

'No!' His hand tightened on mine. 'We have to find an answer that isn't so damned restful. So escapist. When I say I want you with me I mean it – wherever I may be. In new countries, in crowds, everywhere – not just here in the solitude of our home.'

I closed my eyes and let my head fall back on the striped chair cushion. I saw again my mother-in-law's challenging eyes – 'All the time you go deeper into some safe private world of your own where Kobie can't follow you.' Me on the inside, Kobie on the outside?

'Don't press me now,' I pleaded. 'Just get all you can out of this conference and the tour. See everything, hear everything and think how best to use your observations for the benefit of our farmers.'

'I hate to leave you. What'll you do – all alone here?'

'I won't stay here. I'll take Gert to the sea – to Gran. It'll only be a matter of six weeks or so —'

'Perhaps longer, I'll miss you dreadfully.'

'You'll be too busy – too interested. It could even be good for us to have a break from each other —'

'A break. I don't like that word.'

A *break?* Was there, perhaps, something a bit sinister about the word?

❧ 13 ❧

EVERYTHING SEEMED TO HAPPEN AFTER I'D MADE my final decision not to go to America with Kobie.

Before the year was out Gran died of a stroke which, had she lived, would have left her permanently paralysed. The spacious pleasant Muizenberg flat was, of course, bequeathed to my mother, her only child, and I received a generous legacy, a few trinkets of great sentimental value to me and a haunting seascape that she had known I loved. Kobie loved it too. It had been the main feature in the small bedroom always known as 'Jo's room'.

He stood admiring it when he had hung it in our bright living-room with its big landscape window looking out over the bush to the Sneeuberg, amethyst and ethereal now above the shimmer of the heat haze and the illusion of shining water. The sweet scent of the yellow thorn-tree flowers drifted in to us, regardless of the drought.

'This picture has brought the sea to the Karoo,' he said.

'More than that, liefie. It's brought back those wonderful summers when you and I discovered each other and learnt what love was all about. Now, as I look at it, I can hear the surf and the crying gulls . . .'

I had heard them too in those days before the silence had deepened and stilled the voices of nature.

He held me in his arms under the sea picture, as he had so often done in the stolen love hours of long ago, and I wondered, with a tremor of foreboding, if I was a fool not to go with him to America. We had never been parted since our marriage. Was this break – so soon to come – wisdom or madness?

Daddy retired from active business in the New Year and my parents sold up the old house in Main Street, pulled up the roots of over a quarter of a century and moved down to the Cape to the Muizenberg flat where there was still room for Kobie, Gert and me to stay with them for holidays. Maria, as unrestrained as ever in her attire, remained to look after them.

I helped Mummy with the Verfontein end of the move and realised for the first time that Lizzie and Livingstone had grown old in the service of my family. Both were pensioned. The old gardener retired to the Bantu location to end his days with his children and grandchildren, and it fell to me to drive Lizzie to the coloured village with her varied assortment of belongings, most of which had at some time or another belonged to my mother. Her friends and relations ran out of their cottages to help her unload them from the car. Every parcel they deposited on the ground seemed to sever a separate tie with my childhood, I hugged Lizzie, too close to tears for speech, and when I drove away she was standing in a friendly group. Brown hands waved to me, but not Lizzie's. Her little triangular face was all screwed up and the fierce sun picked out the grey in her frizzy mop.

I returned to the old house, empty now, for Mummy and Daddy were spending their last few days at the Verfontein Hotel. I went into the garden and put my arms about the gnarled grey trunk of the familiar fig tree. My dress was sleeveless and, as I closed my eyes and leaned my cheek against the bark, sharply aware of its rough summer warmth, each separate groove and whorl entered my skin and became part of me. For a moment I recovered the transient innocence that precedes expulsion from Eden. Here Kobie, the little boy, so brave – I now knew – so very much a stranger, had mastered his fears and misgivings by fondling the long ears and silky coat of Honey, my spaniel. From my vantage point among the leaves I had seen my dog accept him and make him welcome, so that my hostility was pierced by faith in Honey's instinct. After all, this new child must be all right.

So here, in early childhood, in the dappled light of a hot new year like this one, my destiny had caught up with me.

The ides of March.

Kobie flew to San Francisco from Johannesburg, and I took Gert to Muizenberg to stay with my parents. Mummy had redecorated Gran's flat with gay modern simplicity and it seemed bigger and airier than before. She had glassed in the sun-balcony adjoining my old room to make a sleeping-porch for Gert who was now nearly two and a half. He was a merry little chap with his pale gold curls, mischievous eyes and infectious chuckle and we had hard work preventing Maria from spoiling him.

After the drought-stricken flaky veld soil, where Chief's hooves put up spurts of dust as we cantered across the low bush to the koppie, it was wonderful to walk for miles along the damp, firm, white sands at low tide. Even to exchange the tired fragrance of thorn flowers for the salt tang of the sea was exhilarating. I was glad now that I hadn't gone with Kobie. No efforts need be made here, no attempt to tune in to new sound tracks with a faulty battery.

'Just relax and enjoy this invigorating air,' said Daddy, the evening of our arrival. 'Do you know, Jo, our seasons are changing here in South Africa. Even since I was a boy. Only fifty years ago. Summer comes much later and so does winter. Here it is, the middle of March – the beginning of autumn – and one soft bright day follows another. The sea is full of bathers.'

'When do you expect Kobie back?' asked Mummy. 'We mean to keep you and Gert here till then.'

'Early May. He'll be away about two months. Months – longer than we thought at first. We'd love to stay on here, Mummy.'

'He's lucky his mother and that splendid overseer, Bosman, can take care of the farm. You wouldn't be so good, my girl.' Daddy smiled and gave my long hair a gentle tug.

'I love Springbok Spruit and everything on it, but I'm a passenger. Perhaps, if Ma weren't so competent, I'd pull up my socks. How's Rita?'

'She's coming to dinner tomorrow night, Rob too, if he can get off but that's always questionable.' Mummy's eyes were suddenly reflective. 'I've a feeling that things aren't quite right between those two, Rob's rather tense and Rita's temperamental.'

'They're both overworking,' said Daddy. 'Rita's going to Johannesburg next week for film tests. She could land a leading part in a South African production if she's lucky.'

Rita came next evening, but without Rob.

'He couldn't get off,' she said, shortly. 'He's very disappointed. He was looking forward to this evening and specially to seeing Jo again.'

Her smile was less brilliant than usual, her eyes less sparkling blue. There was a ragged end-of-season weariness about her movements. She's not bothering to act, I thought. What's wrong? But she was, as usual, sweet and laughing with Gert who had waited up for her in his short summer pyjamas.

'This I envy you,' she said to me, as he flung his arms round her neck.

'Get married then. Create a little golden Van der Walt of your own.'

She sighed as she tucked him into bed with his teddy bear and kissed him goodnight.

'How simple you make it sound, Jo-Jo.'

It wasn't simple for Rita. She told me about it when we went for a walk along the beach after dinner. The night was soft and moonlit and our shadows went with us across the firm wet sand where the shellfish burrowed as the wavelets of low tide ebbed. We were barefoot, our denims rolled up above our knees.

'To paddle in the moonlight. Bliss!'

'Bliss?' she echoed. 'I suppose so. To know bliss and hold it and never let it go – that would be wonderful.'

She wasn't thinking of paddling. She was thinking of love.

'Could you tell me what's worrying you? It might help.'

'Rob and I are at the crossroads. I go to Jo'burg next week. He'll come and see me there later – in May perhaps. I think it'll be goodbye. He goes back to Australia in August —'

'August! So soon —'

She stopped in her tracks to stare at me. I felt the colour flame in my cheeks but moonlight drains pink to silver pale. I looked down at the foam swirling harmlessly round our ankles.

'You sound so shocked, Jo.'

'Only surprised. Will you go with him, Rita?'

'Not on his terms.'

'Do you love him?'

We left the sea for the dunes above it. We sprawled there, rolling down the legs of our slacks for the fine dune sand had cooled. The grasses made long spiky shadows.

'There's a French saying, "Il y a toujours l'un qui embrasse et l'autre qui tend la joue" . . . If you want to know about love go to the French —'

'Which are you?'

'The first – the one who loves, not the one who offers the cheek. I make the running. I always have. He needs me. He's very much a man. He offers the cheek all right – and a hell of a lot more – but with curious secret reservations. I asked him once if there was anyone else, and he said, "A man doesn't reach the age of twenty-six without falling in love at some time or another." I asked him if she was free – if he still wanted her . . .'

'What did he say?'

Rita traced an R in the sand, but the grains were too fine and ran in on the letter as if she'd written in water.

'He said, "She's not free . . . and I want you."'

'You've been . . . lovers . . . a long time.' I found it painful to say 'lovers'.

'Since that spring a year and a half ago —'

'At Springbok Spruit when you first came there together?'

'The night we spent in Bloemfontein. Then I didn't see him for months – not till he came to Groote Schuur. After that we were steadies. And now he wants to marry me before he goes home to Australia.'

'You love him. Then marry him.'

'How can I when he offers me a life he well knows I can't and won't accept?'

'You mean he wants to go back to work among the Aborigines in the Northern Territory —?'

'Or any undeveloped Australian dependency that needs medical assistance. Never mind the climate, the primitive conditions, the hopeless isolation or the total unsuitability for a wife and family. Never mind any damn thing, except suffering black humanity. Why, why, *why* can't he exercise his gifts and experience in a city practice? I don't mind going to Australia and doing my own housework and all the rest of it, so long as I've got him with me. I could carry on my own work in a city – on the stage till the babies come, and after that on T.V. and radio. He'd have his career, I'd have a modified version of mine, we'd have each other and a decent home and children. Doesn't that seem a reasonable compromise to you?'

I thought about it before I answered her.

'To you and me – yes,' I said, at last. 'But Rob's different. He doesn't care about making money, or comfort. He cares tremendously about people —'

'Why should he sacrifice himself in lonely, scorching, sweltering outposts when he can help people in civilized circumstances? They're suffering people too!'

'Because there are plenty of clever surgeons willing to help suffering people in civilized circumstances and few enough who'd give up their lives to the hopeless sort of people he wants to help. He wouldn't be sacrificing himself, working *his* way, Rita. He'd be fulfilling himself.'

'He'd be sacrificing me. Surely you must see that!' When I was silent she pressed me further. 'Would *you* do it? Would you go to the end of the world – beyond the black stump, as he puts it – with Rob?'

'I'd realize that you can't change Rob. You'd be pitting yourself against an ideal if you tried – one of the intangibles a woman can't fight and defeat without destroying something rare and wonderful. So, I guess, if I loved him enough – it would need to be a big selfless love – I'd take him on his terms.'

She stared at me angrily, as if I'd betrayed her. As if I'd taken Rob's side in an insoluble dispute. At last she said:

'It was silly of me to ask you that. You're not like a normal young woman. You wouldn't mind isolation and lack of company like I should. You'd have your man to yourself and you could do without the social side of life. It means so little to you in your particular circumstances. Even the theatre is a dead loss to you. How can I expect you to understand?'

Her lovely actress's voice was clear as a bell. It was never hard for me to hear Rita. She spoke with her eyes and lips and hands. She was infinitely expressive. I wondered if she intended to hurt me as much as she did. Her cruel words set me apart from normal youth. She wasn't far wrong at that. I was a write-off, a natural for Rob's 'never-never', the dead heart of Australia 'beyond the black stump'.

❊ 14 ❊

RITA WENT TO JOHANNESBURG FOR HER FILM TESTS.
It was deadlock with her and Rob. Rita found Rob's attitude
unreasonable while he understood hers but stood by his
principles. I was sorry for both of them, but less so for Rita
because Mummy – who was usually no gossip – had talked
about them to me.

'Lately Rita hasn't been going out exclusively with Rob
the way she used to. There's a film director very interested
and he's been taking her here, there and everywhere —'

'For how long?'

'The past month or so.'

'What's he like?'

'Dynamic. About thirty – one of the up-and-coming
Afrikaner intellectuals who's now dabbling in films. Simon
Viljoen —'

'The playwright? Acts in his own shows.'

'That's right. He's a live wire and quite recently he
inherited a fortune. It seems he intends to invest it in making
authentic South African films.'

'Could be useful to Rita.'

'Yes,' said my mother slowly. 'But she isn't really happy.'

'She's an actress. She can act happy when she likes.'

Mummy opened her eyes at me, wide and questioning.

'She wanted Rob,' I said defensively. 'She went full out to get him – and keep him. She could marry him any time. But her career comes first – before love.'

'That's as may be. But, if she's turned him down – whatever her reasons – she's not happy with her decision.'

I shrugged my shoulders. I was still smarting from Rita's last shot at me – relegating me into the never-never. So I was a misfit.

Rob came alone to see us whenever he was free – for a swim or a walk, depending on the weather which continued bright and sunny.

Kobie wrote often and enthusiastically from California. The conference was a tremendous success. He was learning a great deal and on the forthcoming 'field tour' would see and learn still more. His letters were full of his experiences and impressions, and of love too – how much he missed Gert and me. He longed for me to be with him. They rang true as a bell, yet I folded them with an empty feeling. If I were really there he mightn't be as glad to have me as he thought. Who wanted to be saddled with a misfit?

One day, when the sea was cold with a plague of stinging blue-bottles in the surf, Rob took me for a long ramble across the mountain heights above Constantia. The south-easter was rising but the narrow contour path was reasonably protected by the rocky bastions above it.

We paused to look down at the vineyards, and across them to the eastern vleis and lakes near the sea and the far blue mountains beyond, curving round False Bay. The grapes had been gathered and the vines were shedding red and gold leaves; tall rows of poplars swayed dementedly, willows wept thin golden tears and the oaks were afflicted with mildew.

'End of summer,' I said. 'Autumn's a sad season – a transition from life into death.'

His arm tightened round my shoulders.

'Winter isn't death. It's only hibernation – a sleeping period before the excitement and rebirth of spring.'

I turned to look up at him and felt the wind snatch at my hair and whip it back from my lifted face. My body turned towards him too. With the movement the spark always between us flamed high, and the next moment I was caught in his arms. He was saying something against my cheek. I felt the warmth of his mouth and breath but the words were blown away unheard. It didn't matter, his lips now told me wordlessly that he wanted me and had done ever since we'd first met so long ago above the Swan River in far away Perth.

He lifted me as if I were a child – off the path into the shelter of a granite outcrop. I felt the soft grass under my legs and bare midriff between my bolero and shorts, and then the tie that held my bolero was free and my head whirled as Rob's hands sent their burning messages like fever through my skin and veins.

There, out of sight, out of the turbulent wind, out of the whole wide world, in our bowl of warm sunshine protected by tall mountain-mimosa trees, we clung together, our passionate attraction acknowledged at last, refusing to be denied. Acknowledged, but only briefly appeased. Could it ever be really appeased – this hunger awakened so fiercely by the first taste of honey?

The scent of aromatic shrubs and crushed grass was strong and pleasant as we lay at rest under the sky, Rob's bushshirt under my head, his broad chest tanned by the long summer, the lock of black hair falling across his forehead.

'What are you thinking, my darling?' He'd never called me that before. It wasn't Rob's way to throw about the meaningless endearments of most of our group, nor the casual kisses either. I smiled.

'Now, this minute, I was thinking that an hour ago was the first time you've ever kissed me – and we've known each other over three years, on and off.'

'A lot more off than on. It's not the first time I've wanted to – as you well know!'

'But it has to end – here and now. You see that, don't you?'

'I've seen it all along. What happened this afternoon wasn't premeditated. It was just . . . inevitable. It had to be.'

I shivered, suddenly aware that the sun was low and long evening shadows were invading our sanctuary. I sprang to my feet, my body cold and shrinking as a gust of wind penetrated the sturdy mimosa leaves. Flocks of birds were flying overhead, down towards the *vleis* to their night-roosting places.

'It's getting late, Rob. We must go!'

'I can't let you go . . . not now . . .'

'You must – oh, darling, you must!'

I wrenched myself out of his encircling arms. The wind-driven clouds fled in white panic-stricken flocks across the evening sky. Gert's bathtime, his supper, domestic routines – all had been forgotten. Loyalties, obligations, problems great and small had been obliterated by a fleeting elemental interlude of sheer madness.

Was that the sum total of it? Chemical magnetism – irresistible, offered the right circumstances? No more than that? No involvement of heart or spirit? Even so, it could be devastating. But if what had just happened on this lovely mountainside was a flashing red light warning to both of us, it was nothing to the deeper danger contained in the answer to my half-formulated questions – a danger that was to build up fast in the weeks ahead.

When we got back to the flat Mummy had already given Gert his bath and his supper. He was prancing about, merry as a cricket, in his pyjamas and dressing-gown.

'Gert's ready for bed,' she said, 'and we're eating punctually because we're going out at eight —'

'I'm sorry,' I said. 'We didn't know, or we'd have been back earlier. Are you going out to bridge?'

'Yes, to a family game with the Macdonalds.'

'Rob has to get back to Groote Schuur by nine – or is it ten?' I glanced at him and he smiled.

'Split the difference. I'm relieving Alaric Dundas in Casualties at ten. He has some rather special date. He's quite a lad – our Alaric.'

When my parents had gone and Gert was asleep and Maria had said goodnight to us before going to her room across the quadrangle, Rob drew me down on to the couch beside him. The light from a standard lamp fell across his thin bony face and shock of black hair as he pulled on his little pipe.

'D'you mind my smoking a pipe in the sitting-room? I wouldn't do it if your mother was here.'

'Mummy wouldn't mind. Daddy used to smoke a pipe too, but he's been warned off it. Bad for the heart. You should know.'

'A lot of things are bad for the heart. I should know.' His eyes were twinkling but rueful.

I would have liked to rest my head on his shoulder, quietly and in silence. But, when his pipe was well alight, Rob laid it in the big ash-tray and took me firmly by the shoulders, turning me to face him.

'Jo, I want to talk about you – and I want your full attention —'

'You want me to *concentrate?*'

'I do. But you don't have to look cross about it.'

His understanding grin forced an answering smile from me.

'Oh, Rob, it's just that the word concentrate seems to sum up my whole daily life. Other people just talk – quickly, heads turned away, calling across a room or from outside it. Communication is so easy for them. For me it means *concentration*. You've twisted me around so I can watch your lips and your eyes and not miss whatever you want to tell me.'

'That's exactly it, darling. You've put the whole picture very well. Now here's what I want to tell you. It's damned important and I don't propose to let you miss out on any part of it.'

'Fire away.'

'That picture you've just given me with so much feeling .. well, I don't believe it has to stay that way. I believe – though I could be horribly wrong – that it can be brought right back to normal, to the easy come-and-go of casual communication.'

This was not the man who had held me in his arms on the mountain side with the wild wind whirling round us and wild passions sweeping through us. This was Dr Stirling, the surgeon, whose faith lay in the healing knife.

'Go on.'

'There are opportunities in every life – outside chances – that must be recognized and seized. I think one of these chances may have come your way. I don't know for sure, but I hope so.'

I had crouched back against the arm of the couch, my bare feet curled under me – I'd kicked off my mules – my eyes intent upon his face. He was drawing on his pipe as if for inspiration.

'What is this . . . outside chance?' I asked.

'The agricultural conference in San Francisco isn't the only important conference in the world. There are many. There's one right here in Groote Schuur Hospital next week. It's a world congress of ear, nose and throat specialists. James Sherard, a surgeon friend of mine from Sydney, arrived for it today with his wife, Eve. She does his auditory tests.'

He paused. I shook my head.

'I don't know of James Sherard. Should I?'

'You don't – yet. Sydney's a long way from Cape Town. He's youngish. Thirty-four, but already he's recognized in the medical profession as a leading authority on micro-surgery. He has great experience, the highest degrees, and his own technique. The Sherard procedures are being adopted by most top surgeons in his line.'

So here was the opportunity that must be recognized and seized. I said slowly:

'If your friend's here for a congress he won't have time to see private patients, much less operate on them. Anyway, I'm afraid of surgery after my grandmother's experience.'

'This is fairly new surgery, developed in recent years – long after your grandmother's operation. If you turn out to be a suitable case for Sherard's operation – and that's a big *if*, I'm afraid – it could change your whole life.'

Ah, Rob, what prophetic words! Change mine – and what of yours and Kobie's?

'An improvement, you mean? I'd be less deaf?'

'A cure. You could come good, be a girl with normal hearing.'

'No guarantee —'

'There never is in surgery. Anything could go wrong in any field. The point is to weigh the chances —'

'And take a gamble.'

'Find out the odds and make a decision.'

A strange thing was happening to me. This was my grand-mother's room. I was curled up in the corner of her old couch where she'd so often sat with her work-basket open beside her or a crossword puzzle on her knee, deaf to the radio I'd probably be playing. She'd been bravely ahead of her time in trying surgery and it hadn't been a success. Somehow this had created a prejudice in me. A block. Now, as Rob spoke – simply and firmly, raising hopes I hardly dared contemplate, but with caution and no rash promises – I could almost feel her presence close to me. It was as if she whispered, 'Have courage, Jo-Jo. Take a gamble on getting back into the world!'

At last I said:

'How do I manage to consult Dr Sherard?'

'Come to Groote Schuur Hospital at four tomorrow afternoon. I'll meet you inside the main doors. James'll see you, his wife'll do the necessary tests and I'll be with you.'

'Then you've got this all set up already?'

'Yes.'

'You cared enough to think about me, to arrange all this . . .'

'Don't try to measure how much I care about you, darling. Be at Groote Schuur tomorrow at four. That's what matters.'

He rose and knocked out his pipe. He slipped it into the pocket of his old tweed jacket.

'I must hurry. Alaric will be fuming if I'm late. So will his bird.'

But he stayed a moment to stroke my hair, to push it gently back. He touched the two little aids with sensitive fingers.

'You have such pretty ears, small pink shells. Goodnight, Jo . . . my very dear Jo.'

I watched him go – a lean supple dark man with finely carved features, hollowed by overwork.

'Don't try to measure how much I care . . .' he'd said. But I couldn't help trying. This afternoon on the mountainside had been one thing, our talk tonight another. Tonight's sort of caring had been planned with forethought – a proposition put to me carefully. He had made it clear that he might – only *might* – be throwing me a lifeline back to the world and out of the deep silent ocean in which I was drowning without resistance. Was such caring love? No, it was just a particle of his dedication to all who needed help. He would have done as much for any abo in the outback.

But this afternoon? That had been a very different caring – if you could call it such. It had been a wild unreasoning response to the forces of nature. Instinct. Not to be confused with love . . .

I met him at four o'clock next day in the entrance of the huge sprawling hospital. He was very professional in his white coat and he threw me a quick smile of encouragement. If he was at all anxious on my account it was masked by his practical manner.

'Do your parents know about this?'

'No. I didn't want to tell them anything till after Dr Sherard has seen me. Maybe not then. It depends what he has to say.'

'Good,' said Rob. 'Now come along, Jo. This way.'

❧ 15 ❧

MY HEART WAS THUMPING AS I WENT WITH ROB down endless corridors and up in a huge lift.

All night I had tossed and turned as visions of a full life in the world with all its sounds opened before me. I was too young to be the recluse I'd gradually become and the unexpected possibility of a cure had transformed my attitude from resignation to rebellion. If this Australian surgeon could really open the doors of my cage, I'd fly out into freedom like a wild bird, spread my wings and sing! Till yesterday I'd feared the knife. Then Rob had changed all that and now what I dreaded most was a negative verdict. 'If the nerve is impaired,' Rob had explained, 'it'll be no go. We must keep our fingers crossed.' The day was chilly and I was a mass of apprehensive shivers.

At last he opened a door into a light, rather bare room. There was a desk, a filing cupboard, a table with an instrument tray on it and one of those high narrow couches covered with a white sheet.

A stocky youngish man with short-cropped red hair and a pleasant grin rose from the chair behind the desk and Rob introduced us.

'Mrs Van der Walt, nice to meet you. My wife'll be with us in a minute.'

I could see that James Sherard was speaking up, and I tried to match his easy friendly approach, but my nerves were taut as bowstrings.

Rob didn't delay. He said, 'I'll leave Jo in your hands, James. See you in about an hour's time.'

Mr Sherard nodded a cheerful dismissal to Rob and offered me a chair.

'I'm going to ask you some personal questions, Mrs Van der Walt. Do your best to answer them. It won't be all that easy. Certain things are difficult to pinpoint.'

His hands – I always notice hands – were blunt and quick, immaculately kept. He took up a pencil and tapped it on the blotter. A notepad with my name and the date on it lay open on the desk. I gave my mind to listening to his abrupt questions and somehow this effort helped to calm me.

'Your age?' His light brown eyes, like clever pebbles, were amused. '*You* won't mind answering that one! Some do.'

'Twenty-three.'

'When did you first notice that you had a hearing problem?'

I frowned. 'It's hard to say. I think other people spotted it before I did. Even then . . . Well, in my last year at school I lost ground, I'd been high in class before that . . .'

'You weren't hearing your teachers properly?'

'I guess it was that. But my school reports put a different

construction on it. The comments suggested that my mind was on my boyfriend instead of my work.'

'And was it?'

I smiled. 'Sure. I married him soon after I left school.'

He laughed. 'There are always red-herrings. Your boy-friend was one. Can you recall just when *you* began to worry?'

'Very well indeed. We had a baby girl. She died when she was only a few weeks old. She was in the next room to ours with the door wide open, yet she choked to death and I didn't wake. There must have been some little sound – something that should have alerted me.'

'Didn't your husband hear anything?'

'Nothing. But he sleeps soundly and works out of doors all day.'

'Just the same, his not being disturbed or hearing anything that night was red-herring number two. Now, tell me, has anyone in your family had this trouble?'

'My grandmother. She had it when she was a teenager, and it got worse after my mother was born. She had an operation. It didn't work.'

'How long ago was that operation?'

'Oh, heavens – in the dim dark ages! When she was still quite young.'

'I thought so. Now there are some auditory tests my wife will give you. After that I'll see you again ... Eve, meet Mrs Van der Walt.'

An attractive fair woman had come into the room. She was probably in her early thirties. Slim and boyish. She held out her hand to me and her smile was warm and encouraging, as if she knew and sympathized with my inner hopes and anxieties. But her husband's rather brusque manner had done much to steady me.

Eve Sherard led me into the adjoining room.

'It's sound-proofed,' she explained, as she placed me in a chair by a desk covered with electrical equipment. 'There's no interference here. Now I'm going to put these earphones on your head and you must tap on my desk every time you hear a signal.'

As I tapped, she filled in a graph form.

'There, that's enough of that. Just one more test.' She took away the two earphones and replaced them with a single instrument fitted to a headband. 'A sort of Cyclops eye – or rather, ear – right in the middle of your forehead. Now, when you hear the signals, tell me which ear they sound in . . . Well done. Now I'll take this graph to James and he'll study it before examining you himself. Would you like a cup of tea while you wait?'

'Love it.'

'Good. I won't be long.' She was gone before I could ask her what she thought of my chances.

I was glad to be alone for a few minutes. So often Kobie or Mummy had begged me to concentrate more. This afternoon my concentration had been stretched to its limit. She brought a tray with tea and biscuits and set it on the big desk.

'Help yourself, my dear. I have some work to do for my

husband, so I must leave you. I'll call you as soon as he's ready.'

The surgeon's examination was brief. I lay on the high couch and he applied delicate tuning forks to the back of each ear against the bone. I indicated the onset and fading of faint quivering vibrations. Then he looked down each ear with a long instrument with a light attached to it. He straightened up and smiled down at me.

'That's the lot, Mrs Van der Walt.'

I sat up and got my little hearing-aids out of my bag and fixed them in place. Whatever he said next was going to set the course of my life – inwards towards isolation, or out to the world. I found myself suddenly cold and shivery.

He was already standing at his desk making notes when I went, rather shakily, and sat where I could face him.

The clever pebble eyes were warmly pleased.

'It's otosclerosis – as Rob thought. Operable. The betting on a complete cure by means of surgery is ten to one. Do you want to take that chance?'

'I can't wait to take it – if *you* will operate.'

'I can only operate under certain conditions, Mrs Van der Walt. My time is very limited. You'd have to allow me to use you as a demonstration case for this congress. You'd need to make a rather quick decision. I understand your husband's in America. You'll want to discuss this with him. You might prefer to wait till he gets back and have a South African surgeon —'

'When I told you I couldn't wait, I meant it, Mr Sherard. When will you want me as a demonstration case?'

'You'll need to come to this hospital on Thursday evening. I'll do your stapedectomy on Friday morning. You'll be in the ward for the weekend. On Monday you'll go home and I'll remove your dressings the following Friday. The whole thing may take a few weeks to settle down completely. After that you should be on your way. Any questions?'

I tried to subdue my excitement and think intelligently. Today was Monday. Only a few days to wait! I steadied my voice.

'If it fails – if I'm the unlucky one out of ten – will I be worse off than I am now?'

'No. You'll still be able to use your aid. We do your worst ear first – the left – and, if, later on, you want the other done as well you can go ahead with that. It's up to you.'

'What is this . . . otosclerosis? What's been happening to me in the past few years to make me so deaf?'

'It's an outcrop of bone – let's call it rogue bone. It goes wild, it invades and extends your own healthy bone till it covers the window through which you should hear and immobilizes the stapes —'

'The stapes?'

'A tiny stirrup-shaped bone that should be free in your ear like the tongue of a bell. If you tied the tongue of a bell to its wall it would cease to ring. That's what's happened to you.'

'So you free it?'

'I chip away the bad bone and replace the damaged stapes with a new one. It's tiny – no bigger than a matchhead.'

'Is the bad bone likely to grow again?'

'I haven't known it do so.'

There was one more question. The answer would mean a great deal to Kobie and me. We wanted another son – for ourselves, for Gert, for Springbok Spruit.

'Would another pregnancy – just one more – wreck the whole job?'

He studied my face thoughtfully.

'It shouldn't affect the ear on which I'll operate.'

'I understand. The other might deteriorate. If so, I can have it done too – later on.'

'Right.'

'Life is all risks, isn't it?'

He grinned. 'And no insurance covers the lot. Now, tell me, have you any allergies you know of? Any tendency to bleeding?'

'I don't think so. There were no complications when I had my babies.'

'Would you mind a local anaesthetic? The operation takes about half an hour. It's not painful – just some rather odd noises that I'll explain as I work. Of course, if you're nervous you can have a general.'

'Which do you advise?'

'Local, in your case.'

'I'd prefer it too. My babies were born the natural way. I co-operated in giving them birth. To me this would be a bit the same – co-operating in my own rebirth.'

He looked startled – as if, for a moment, he feared I might be setting my hopes too high. Then he nodded and smiled.

'We'll go ahead on those lines, Mrs Van der Walt. Ah, here's Eve – and Rob.'

As Eve came into the room with Rob, James Sherard rose and patted his friend on the back.

'It's all fixed, mate. Friday morning. Okay?'

'Very much so! Thanks a million, James.'

Rob's eyes were shining as he grabbed my arm. I noticed that he had discarded his white coat and was in an ordinary suit.

'I'm going home with you, Jo. We'll tell your parents and phone Kobie.'

I walked on air with Rob down those long corridors and out into the blustery autumn evening.

❧ 16 ❧

ROB EXPLAINED EVERYTHING TO MY PARENTS WHILE
I sat in a sort of dream world, Gert on my knee sleepily
turning over the pages of an animal picture book.

'We must hope it will go well,' said Mummy, still doubtful because of Gran. But Daddy was wholeheartedly for the
operation.

'We must put a call through at once to Kobie in San
Francisco,' he said. 'It's seven here, it'll be somewhere
around lunchtime there. Anyway it'll be a civilized hour to
get him.'

'I wish I could speak to him myself,' I said, 'but I'm bad
on the 'phone and hopeless on long distance when I get in a
flap. Whatever happens, I don't want him even to think of
coming back or cutting his tour short.'

'I'll speak to him.' Daddy's tone was firm. 'Then Rob can
chip in and tell him anything he wants to know about Mr
Sherard and this microsurgery.'

The call came through just after we'd finished dinner.

We clustered round the telephone as Daddy spoke.

'Kobie, Jo is here next to me. We have exciting news for
you. Something very important.' He went on to tell Kobie
about the surgical congress at Groote Schuur and James

Sherard. 'He's a friend of Rob's from Sydney, an authority on a certain operation that should be able to restore Jo's hearing . . . Yes, yes, we all know about Gran. This is different, a very much more recent technique . . . Wait, I'll hand you over to Rob. He'll explain.'

Rob took the receiver. My eyes were riveted on his face. I saw it change from eagerness to dismay at whatever Kobie was saying. At last he cut in sharply:

'But Kobie, you don't seem to get me. I know Jo refused surgery with the Johannesburg specialist. The fact is she's changed her mind. Sherard's a world authority in this type of microscopic surgery. He's examined Jo and finds her a suitable subject in every way. He's demonstrating his method on Friday and he's offered to operate on Jo . . . Yes, use her for the demonstration. What's wrong with that? . . . No, it's not a long business. Half an hour under local, two or three days in hospital . . . How does she feel about it? She's mad keen – can't wait . . . Hold on a moment! She says I'm to tell you in no circumstances to hurry back. It's quite pointless. The quieter she keeps for her convalescence the better . . .'

I could hear a sort of mumble over the 'phone. Could Kobie be making serious objections?

Rob turned to me, his expression incredulous. He relayed my husband's remarks.

'He wants you to wait till he gets back. Then he suggests you have your Johannesburg specialist perform the operation when he can be with you.'

I flung back my head, angry and upset.

'But *why*? Daddy, you take over from Rob! Tell Kobie

this is my decision, no one else's, and I won't delay this operation by so much as an hour! And Sherard is the surgeon I want. I'm not asking Kobie's advice. I'm simply informing him of what is going to happen. Tell him to stick to his plans at all costs, and I'll stick to mine. That's all.'

I heard my father do as I asked, expressing my views less arrogantly – like an adept interpreter.

When he put down the receiver after saying, 'Goodbye then, Kobie, we'll keep in touch. Jo sends her love,' he turned to me thoughtfully.

'Is it all right?' I asked.

'Yes.'

'What was that last thing Kobie said to you?'

Daddy hesitated. Then he braced his shoulders and looked down at me with a half smile in his dark eyes.

'He said, "If Jo prefers Rob's opinion to mine, that's up to her."'

'Of course I do in this case!'

He patted my hand as he added, 'Go ahead with your plan, my child. We're all with you. I guess Kobie just feels rather helpless and far away and out of it. He wants to be with you through this . . . later, after he gets back —'

'Well, that can't be. I won't miss this opportunity.'

Mummy telephoned Ma at Springbok Spruit. She too was all for it. Mummy asked her to cable or ring Kobie and tell him so and to reassure him that there was no danger and he was not to interrupt his tour.

I walked with Rob to his car and we stood for a few

minutes in the night air that smelt of the sea, cold and invigorating.

'You've made one of the big decisions of your life today,' he said. 'I'm sorry I was the one who had to set the wheels in motion – not Kobie.'

I shook my head. Suddenly I was mortally tired.

'Never mind. I'm grateful, Rob. As Ma would say, "Alles sal reg kom" – everything will come right.' But I was no longer sure.

I raised my face and he kissed my lips. I stood under the street lamp and watched him drive away.

Rob was with me on Thursday afternoon when I was admitted to Groote Schuur Hospital. He took me to the European Women's Surgical ward and introduced me to the sister in charge who was surprisingly young and rather pretty.

'I'll leave you with Sister,' he said. 'But I'll pop in again before you go to sleep.'

I nodded, speechless. In spite of my confidence in James Sherard I was apprehensive and emotional. If anything went wrong – if I turned out to be one of the unlucky subjects who ended up 'no worse off' – what would Kobie do? Would he hold me tight and say, 'Ag, liefie, I love you just the same . . .' Yes, but he'd reproach Rob bitterly for raising false hopes as high as the sky.

Sister led me to a small ward for two.

'With any luck you may have it to yourself for the weekend, Mrs Van der Walt. A patient went home today and her bed isn't booked till Monday.'

I could see that she was raising her voice, but it sounded very faint to me in spite of the little 'bubbles'. Without them the silence lately had been total.

The light, airy room was filled with flowers. From my parents, Ma, Rob, and one particularly lovely vase of Peace roses from Kobie. He knew Peace was my favourite flower. His 'Good Luck' cable was propped up against it.

'From my husband,' I said, opening the gold greetings envelope.

'GOD BE WITH YOU' I read. 'WISH I WAS TOO WITH ALL MY LOVE   KOBIE'

I put it back in its envelope by the roses and with the gesture my fit of nervous depression lifted. I smiled at Sister.

'I washed my hair this morning. Mrs Sherard told me to. And no lacquer.'

'Good.' She touched it. 'We don't cut it or anything. Just tuck it into a sterile shower-cap. You'll be as pretty after your op as you are right now.'

When I was in bed a ward maid brought me a light supper and soon afterwards the Sherards came together to see me. They didn't stay long. Mr Sherard told me what to expect in the theatre and reassured me.

'We'll see you right, Jo. You're Rob's friend, I can't go on calling you Mrs Van der Walt.'

Eve said: 'Sleep well. The night sister'll give you a tablet to look after that. Happy dreams.'

I laughed. She talked to me as if I were Gert. I rather liked it – just for tonight.

When they had gone, Rob came in. There was such warmth and confidence in his face as he looked at me that my heart lifted.

'Scared, Jo?'

'Not a bit. Will there be students and doctors goofing round the operating table?'

He laughed.

'There's a giant microscope with two eyes for James to look through – like binoculars – and a third eye like a telescope. The camera will look down that and what it sees will be shown on a closed circuit T.V. screen, and everything James says to you as he goes along – explaining what's happening – will form part of the running commentary. There'll be no one in the theatre except James and Eve, a theatre sister and you, and – if you want it – me.'

'I want it more than anything. But then you won't see the T.V. picture.'

'It can be re-run whenever required. But, in any case, I've watched through the telescope several times when James has been operating. That's why I know he's the tops.'

When he left me I felt composed and content. I was no longer worried that Kobie had had other ideas about my surgery at first. He was always impetuous and he liked to be the one responsible for decisions – especially after my deafness increased. I understood his resentment that it was Rob who'd taken the initiative and who was, in a way, in charge. Ever since that night in Verfontein, when he'd seen me dancing with Rob as if we were 'welded together', his easily inflamed sexual jealousy had been aroused and, because he was highly sexed himself, he assumed Rob – and me – to be the same. Maybe he was right, at that! I smiled to myself. Kobie would be so happy when he found himself no longer handicapped by a deaf wife but able to be proud of a young gay woman who'd know what she was laughing about, instead of just reflecting the expressions of other people amused or interested by some remark or story. Oh, how I longed to make the scene again – to join in! More than that, we might have another baby. I slept well.

Early next morning Sister gave me an injection and quite soon I began to feel drowsy and relaxed. My eyes closed. Then a touch on my wrist made me open them again. Rob smiled as he took my pulse.

'How are you feeling? Nice and restful?'

'I've had an injection. I'm sleepy.'

'Good. See you in the theatre.'

The theatre was large and air-conditioned and the powerful light over the operating table on which I lay seemed bigger than a searchlight to me.

James Sherard and Eve were there, capped, gowned and masked. So was Rob. The theatre sister gently turned my head sideways and placed a green cloth over it with a slot to expose my ear. A steel frame on the right side of the operating table kept the cloth off my face.

'Turn your face to the right,' said Eve. 'That's right. Are you quite comfy?'

Under the cloth frame I could see the white theatre wall with a big clock on it, the hands pointing to nine o' clock.

I could also see the tall white stand of the great microscope with its arm trained across the head of the operating table. So this is it, I thought, through my drowsy haze.

I felt James put the speculum into my ear.

'Now for a sharp little prick as I give you the injection,' he said very clearly. 'After that you'll feel me working and you'll hear some cracks and bangs and funny noises. Don't let them worry you. *Nothing will hurt.*'

Suddenly the lights went out and the theatre was very quiet and dark except for the single beam shining into the microscope and on to the instrument tray. Rob peeped under my cloth shelter and made a thumbs up sign.

'Now we're in business,' said James.

I could feel his left hand steady against the side of my head and his right hand using the tiny little instruments that made such curious noises in my head. Perhaps for my sake – more likely for the benefit of the surgeons watching the T.V. screen – he explained every stage as the operation progressed and he chipped away the 'rogue bone' that entombed my hearing and ruined a delicate God-given transmission system.

Although many of the sounds were nerve-racking – such as tappings that appeared to be loosening my teeth! – other exterior noises began to weave through them; James's voice, strangely cavernous but increasingly clear, a word from Rob or Eve, the slight sound of some minute instrument being replaced on the tray, the soft hum of the air-conditioner.

The long hand of the wall clock had moved to half past nine.

Sister removed the cloth and James Sherard came round to talk to me.

'All right, Jo?'

I heard him perfectly!

'All right.'

'Splendid. Everything went according to plan. No surprises or tricky bits. Eve and I have to get back to the conference now, but we'll be in to see you later this morning. You'll hear nicely for a couple of hours; then a blood clot will form and you'll need your aid again till it shrinks. That'll take about a week. Then I'll remove your dressings – a matter of less than a minute. Just take everything as it comes. Don't fuss or bother.'

'Are you shouting?'

'Good heavens, no! Why should I?'

He had taken off his mask, his eyes were polished pebbles, alert and friendly, and his grin was boyish.

Back in the ward which I still had to myself, I lay in a sort of trance. The window was open, the sun streamed in and from De Waal Drive I could hear the swish of tyres and the busy roar of traffic rounding the bend. Tugs hooted in the bay. Alarming, unfamiliar, shocking, glorious! A window rattled as the wind rose. Years since I had heard these things. Only now did I begin to comprehend the full extent of my own past deafness. A new fantastic happiness and relief pervaded me. I was back with the noises of the world. How wonderful!

There was another sound. Footsteps came along the corridor. Firm, a long stride – yes, it had to be Rob.

He stood at my bedside. I looked at him with all the wonder of my rediscovered world in my eyes.

'I *heard* your footsteps. I knew they must be yours! I've never heard them before yet I recognised them . . .'

The wooden stool scraped as he drew it out and sat beside me. He took my hands and pressed them against his cool bony cheek.

'You've come good, Jo – you've come good, my darling.'

'Did you say that loud?'

'I whispered it.'

'Rob, oh, Rob . . . It's a miracle!'

Tears poured down my cheeks. He took a tissue from a box on the bedside table and put it into my hand. Without a word he turned and left me.

I was alone with my indescribable joy – weeping with happiness.

On Sunday night Rob drove me home. By then I was deaf again as James had said I would be.

The second stage of the miracle was performed on the following Friday when James took out the dressing and examined my ear.

'All just as it should be.'

Eve and Rob were with us in the consulting-room where I had first met them. They looked so glad for me. But James warned me that for a while everything would sound strange and often frightening.

'Sounds may echo in your head like cries in an empty house. That will pass as things settle down. Many noises you've forgotten may scare you. You'll soon get used to them again. The world is a very noisy place, Jo. You're back in it.'

'That's what I want. To be back in it!' In the tide of life, buffeted perhaps, but no longer isolated.

'I suggest putting a light sound-resistant plug in your ear for a day or two, so you can adjust gradually.'

'No! I'll take it as it is and really live again.'

Their voices did indeed echo as if in a cave. Rob's deep and resonant, James Sherard's lighter and Eve's low-pitched.

Outside, when Rob drove me home, I had to control sheer terror.

The noises seemed deafening – or so anybody else would say. To me the word 'deafening' has a different meaning. The traffic and the stormy weather! They assaulted the newly opened door of my ear and rushed at that sensitive threshold from all directions as if to burst into my head and create havoc there. It was mad and Wagnerian – a sort of Götterdämmerung of sound. The rain and the wind thundered out of the heavens like the galloping Valkyries. Cars, vans and motor-bikes whooshed, roared, growled, whined, hooted and snarled in a mechanical cacophony I had long forgotten. No wonder wheels were the killers of today. Listen to them! Each noise was a separate threat to which the hard-of-hearing are oblivious. Often, on foot, I had risked my life inadvertently, and horns had blared, teeth gnashed and fists shaken in fury at the stupidity of the 'jay-walker' impeding the path of speed and the power of the man at the wheel.

My heart thumped as I realized that soon I must prepare to plunge into all this turmoil and drive my car again, not just with hands, feet and eyes, but with ears alert to every warning.

'It's quite a thing, isn't it?' said Rob.

'Shocking. And to think I used to drive in it – not realizing —'

'Does it frighten you now?'

'Yes, but I want it. Having babies frightened me, but I wanted them. You can ride your fear, if it's worth the risk.'

It was the same in the quiet flat.

Mummy and Gert met us at the door. My little son's footsteps, scampering across the polished floor of the hall, were like the hooves of a wild pony, and his cry of welcome was as penetrating as a steam whistle when he flung himself upon me.

'Mom! Mom! Can you hear?'

I knelt on the doormat, remembering even then, James Sherard's advice not to make hasty movements with my head. Gert was in my arms and I was hugging him.

'I can hear, darling. You need never shout at me again!'

As we went into the sitting-room, Mummy said: 'I'm just getting tea. Maria's always out at this time, as you know.'

I'd forgotten the clear purity of her voice. Daddy's was mellow, as a tenor's should be.

'You'll have to sing for me again, Daddy,' I said.

He shook his head. 'My singing days are done, Jo-Jo.'

I noticed then how grey his hair had grown, and linked my arm in his.

'You'll have to let me be the judge of that. Heavens! I can hear the kettle boiling and the fridge has just turned itself on.'

After tea, when I went to the bathroom, the sound of rushing water terrified me. Niagara, no less!

'It's not a very peaceful world, is it?' grinned Rob.

We went to the sea-facing window. The rain had ceased and the pale sunlight touched the far mountains. The traffic noises here were thinner and more relaxed, and there was background music, profound and turbulent as the rollers crashed on the long silver beaches. Gulls cried raucously. Behind me I could distinguish the clatter of cups and saucers as Mummy cleared away the tea things. *I could discriminate between different sounds once more!*

I felt Gert's little head pressed against my skirt. I stroked the silky fair curls absently.

'What is it, Mom?' he asked shrilly.

'Ssh, love, not so loud. I'm listening to the great big roar of the sea at high tide. And gulls . . . and you.'

A new sound intruded. The telephone bell. There was a delay, then Daddy called: 'Jo, it's San Francisco. Come and speak to Kobie.'

For a moment I hesitated. The telephone had been one of my bugbears. Rob gave me a little push.

'Don't funk it. Don't funk anything.'

So I went to the 'phone and picked up the receiver, my heart thumping. I heard my husband's voice across half a world.

'Jo, liefie, can you really hear me?'

I gulped, tears smarted in my eyes.

'Kobie, I hear you as if you were with me in this room.'

'Thank God . . . I can't believe it! Will you come to me? I want you with me, Jo-Jo.'

'I can't, darling. I have to keep quiet a while. When you come home in a few weeks' time we'll start a new life together – everything so much easier for both of us.'

He accepted that.

But the new life . . . 'so much easier for both of us'? No signposts told us where that would lead.

PART THREE

Jo, Rob and Kobie

§ 17 §

MA HAD TOLD RITA THE GOOD NEWS AND SHE
telephoned me from Johannesburg genuinely delighted for
my sake. She had good news of her own too. She had landed
the lead in Simon Viljoen's film.

'It means I'll be stuck in Johannesburg for weeks – probably months – but it's the chance of a lifetime. How's Rob?
I miss that wretched man.'

'He's overworking as usual – like everybody else on the
hospital staff. Otherwise all right.'

'Otherwise all right . . . ' she sighed. 'I was afraid so . .
When do you expect Kobie back?'

'A month today he flies in to Johannesburg from somewhere in Texas.'

'Then you must meet him here. Persuade Rob to come
too.'

'I think we could do that. The Sherards —'

'Your super surgeon and his wife?'

'Yes – they're coming to Springbok Spruit to spend a few
days before going back to Australia. Rob's taking a week
off. He's bringing them to the farm and we'll all go on to
Jo'burg together. There it'll be a case of forty-eight hours
of meetings and partings.'

'So it all overlaps. Kobie arrives, the Sherards go home, and if I can get to Jo'burg too, Rob and I can wind up some unfinished business. I only wish I could join you all at Springbok Spruit, but it's not on. We work slave hours in this job.'

She didn't sound tired but exhilarated. Only when she spoke of Rob did her voice hold a trace of sadness, though she was obviously trying to keep it light.

Rob.

During the next three weeks we saw each other whenever possible.

As once Kobie had taught me to drive on quiet country roads, so Rob now did the opposite. With me at the wheel we plunged into the traffic whirl of Cape Town to accustom me to the savagery of the city's roar in the rush hour. As Kobie had often urged the family to raise their voices when speaking to me, Rob persuaded my parents and even Gert to lower their tone considerably. He watched over my convalescence as much as he was able to. Day by day I regained confidence and normal hearing. I adjusted gradually to the hubbub and pace of city life; away from it, at the sea, I fell into a strange mood of dreamy rapture.

How lovely to be able to join in a general conversation without strain – not to have to ask people to repeat themselves! I was emancipated. Chains had fallen from my spirit. They say if one sense fails others take its place. I discovered another truth. The recovery of my hearing enhanced all my other senses. The world about me was brighter, more beautiful and poignant.

How can I describe it? I believe there are drugs that heighten perception. Colours appear more brilliant and luminous, simple objects assume auras of prismatic light, normal sensations cross a magic threshold and take on acute intensity; the spirit floats upwards free of the bodily cage which it regards objectively from the shimmering blue of infinity. I had taken no drug, yet every aspect of life seemed endowed with a new dimension and significance. I could see and feel myself changing. I was ecstatically aware of the fact that I was young and attractive. No longer a misfit . . .

One Sunday Rob drove Gert and me to a lovely spot he had discovered by a waterfall in a mountain kloof. We had to walk up a little way, but Rob carried Gert pick-a-back and I took the picnic basket. The air was sweet with the scent of autumn heath and of the cool peaty water foaming over the fern-covered rockface. Occasionally a golden leaf drifted down from a tree.

'A flutterby!' cried Gert, as he caught one and was disappointed to find that it was only a desiccated leaf he held in his hand.

After lunch, while Gert sprawled on his tummy and dabbled in a rock pool in search of tadpoles, I lay on the grass and let all the old-new sounds seep into my consciousness. That month of April was an Indian summer, warm and languorous at midday but fresh and keen before sunrise and after sunset. Those four weeks in which I returned to life were idyllic, a period entranced, unfolding one revelation after another.

Rob sat beside me, hands clasped about his bare knees, his

back against a sun-warmed boulder, his attention on Gert. Lucky my son was with us, I thought, the memory of a windy afternoon on the mountain suddenly so vivid that it set every nerve tingling. That day, when I was still deaf, had led to this. Now I knew myself to be more than ever vital, even more vulnerable to the forces of nature. We had tried to resist them, to avoid the inflammable situations we could so easily have created. He'd be gone soon – in August – and that would be the end of that.

'You're very quiet,' he said. 'Except for the sigh. Surely no sad thoughts? Listen, Jo, and tell me what you hear.'

'I hear the waterfall and the sharp high calls of the sugar-birds. Gert's swishing his hand in the pool, you're striking a match. Imagine it – such small sounds! The faint rustle of the bell-grasses and leaves whispering in the breath of a breeze . . . it's magical . . . and all thanks to you —'

'To James.'

'Without you, it would never have happened.'

'Sooner or later you'd have got around to it.'

I wondered. He couldn't know what a long distance I'd already travelled away from the world into the deep silence of self. He couldn't know about the U-turn? Yet, with one decisive movement, he'd picked me off my solitary road.

'Have you got leave to come to Springbok Spruit next month with the Sherards?' I asked.

'I think it'll be on.'

'And then Johannesburg. Rita wants to see you there.'

'She'll be on location in Swaziland.'

'She'll get to Jo'burg somehow.'

168

'What's the good? She can't change me and I can't change her. We called it a day when Simon Viljoen crooked his finger and she followed him.'

'She's had time for reflection. I think – after her fashion – Rita really loves you.'

He shook his head. 'I don't delude myself, Jo. She loves the man she'd like me to be. A successful city surgeon who can offer her security, a home and children – and the possibility of continuing her career.'

'She'd leave her own country and go with you to yours. She'd fit in anywhere and make friends easily —'

'She'd fit into any background that could advance her ambitions. She wouldn't fit in with heat, flies, droughts, floods, isolation and backward humanity —'

'She'd have you.'

He grinned ruefully and puffed at his pipe.

'Small compensation. She's young, gay and gifted. Can you blame her for refusing to sacrifice her ambitions for a bunch of primitive folk she doesn't even know about? I can't. But I have a . . . sort of . . . vocation. I can't go back on it. We were honest with each other from the word go.'

'She might have thought she was, but deep down I bet she hoped to change you.'

He rose and went to kneel beside Gert at the pool. Over his shoulder he said: 'There's nothing like hard work for making people forget their mistakes.'

'Is experience – even emotional experience – ever a mistake?'

He turned and stood over me where I lay in the speckled shadow of a mountain acacia.

'Answer your own question, my darling.'

I sat up, the blood hot in my cheeks and throat, my heart thumping. I began to pack up the picnic basket.

'There's a cup missing.'

'Your son has it. He hoped to catch a tadpole.'

'Well, I need the cup. So his hopes must be dashed.'

Rob laughed as he lifted my indignant son from the water's edge, still clinging to the empty cup.

'That's makes two of us,' he said. 'Come along, Gert. Mom's the boss – the dasher of foolish hopes.'

Truth is what I have to unearth in writing this story of my personal miracle that was so splendidly launched and came whirling back to strike more than one of us. What transformed it into a boomerang? *What?*

I've turned it over in my mind endlessly through sleepless nights and despairing days.

Circumstances building up to a sort of nemesis? If this? If that?

If drought hadn't stricken the Karoo at the very moment of nation-wide economic crisis would Kobie have felt it necessary to attend a world conference on the future of agriculture? If I had had the courage to go with him? If James Sherard hadn't come from Sydney to Cape Town just then and if Rob hadn't known him and his reputation personally? If he hadn't persuaded me that James Sherard was the best ever to help me? If I'd agreed to wait for Kobie's return and be content with one of our own surgeons? If Rita hadn't broken with Rob and gone to Johannesburg? If that particular magnetism had never been kindled between Rob and me? Even if those last weeks of autumn had been less golden, less warm and bright, things might have worked out differently.

Of course I know that my hearing problem was the cause of all that followed. It both distorted and soldered the peculiar link between a man and a woman already strongly physically attracted. Pity and understanding had been the extra factors on Rob's side, and on mine profound gratitude which built up to a sentiment I believed to be love. Through Rob's initiative I'd regained untold delights – a line of human communication no longer scrambled and the special joys of nature's sounds and calls. I wasn't a city girl. I belonged to a lonely plateau where every sound of bird, beast, insect, or of the elements that could make or destroy us, had meaning for me. It was Rob who slowly taught me to live fully again. Perhaps to him I was like Eliza Dolittle to Professor Higgins. My dependence had for the moment shifted from Kobie to Rob. A different sort of dependence. Now I was on my way forward and outwards instead of back and inwards.

Before we went to Springbok Spruit I had a final auditory test with Eve. She and James were delighted with the result. I had indeed 'come good'.

On the following day Rob, Gert and I, followed by James and Eve in a hired car, drove up through the Hex River valleys and mountains to the Karoo. Although the bush was dry and dusty and the parched earth cracked, the autumn air sparkled with that unpolluted quality so bracing to tired or afflicted lungs.

My mother-in-law, alerted as ever by our dust cloud as we turned into the winding dirt track off what James called 'the bitumen' or 'the black', was on the stoep of the homestead to greet us.

'You're all to stay here,' she said, when the introductions had been performed. 'Jo and Gert too. Jo's house has just been repainted and it needs a little longer to lose that painty smell.'

Our few days sped by. We played tennis and rode and one morning it was hot enough to swim in the pool. Our boreholes were holding out and though the grass round the house was tawny, the roses bloomed and exotic aloes and succulents were beginning to brighten up the rockeries. The lemon and orange trees still yielded fruit and even put out belated blossoms to scent the air.

Ma could hardly credit the change in me.

'It's a transformation!' she said to James. 'You didn't know her before, but she was creeping further and further into her shell. My son will come back to a new young wife – a girl full of the joy of life!'

The day before the four of us went on to Johannesburg, Rob and I drove in to Verfontein alone. The Sherards were out riding, Gert was with Ma and Christabel, and I had my household shopping to do at the Zebra Supermarket.

When he and I had carried my clobber back to the parked car, he said:

'Let's walk down Main Street and take a look at your old

home – and afterwards we'll have lunch at the pub where you and I first danced together.'

Our white house with its teak shutters had been painted Mediterranean pink. The black cast-iron railings were pink too. It no longer looked like the nineteenth-century colonial home it really was. The hotel too had sloughed off its old skin. We sat over coffee in the redecorated lounge with extremely modern furnishings and vases of artificial flowers.

'All very up-to-date,' said Rob. 'So much has changed in eighteen months.'

'Me – most of all.'

'Not really. You're a flowering tree that's just burst into bloom. I knew it could happen. But I never guessed how lovely – how breathtaking – it would be.'

'Tomorrow . . . tomorrow night in Johannesburg . . . Will Rita be there?'

'Not till the next day.'

'She and Kobie – they arrive on the same day then? He from America. She from Swaziland. It won't be easy —'

'Not for you and me. Rita and I – well, that's broken up already. She's coming to see her brother . . . and you – the new Jo without any problem —'

'No problem? Ah, Rob!'

'Rita's about to be a film star with the big boss in her pocket. We shouldn't worry about Rita. She's on her way – the way she's always meant to go. But you, darling . . . Be thankful that in August you'll wash this man right out of your lovely hair.'

'How can I? After what there's been —'

'After tomorrow what there's been between you and me has to be forgotten. It *must* be, Jo! The slate has to be wiped clean . . . ready for a new beginning.'

He meant it. He really did. And I knew that he was right. Every day I found it more difficult to dissemble. Suddenly I said:

'Do you think they guess about us – my parents?'

'Not your mother.'

'And Daddy?'

'He knows his fellow man better than your mother does. He has insight and imagination; he's guided by no set of rules except the manual of common humanity.'

'What's your set of rules, Rob?'

'A very small one. It contains the basic principles, but I can't always live up to them. The Hippocratic Oath lays down the lot for my profession, and it's good enough to cover daily life too. So are the Ten Commandments, come to that, but we all slip up, sooner or later.'

I looked at him as though I feared never to see him again – the dark head so finely drawn against the garish mustard-coloured wall of the hotel lounge, the strong column of the neck, the broad shoulders, the hands I loved. I said:

'I have the feeling sometimes that I'm living in a dream. It's a wonderful dream. I'm afraid of waking.'

When we got back to Springbok Spruit Ma met us – not at the homestead but at my own home where Rob and I were unloading my household purchases in the kitchen and stocking up the fridge and the pantry.

'Kobie telephoned just after you left. He was speaking from New York.'

'Ma! Is anything wrong?'

'Of course not, Jo. But he says he wants to come straight home – here – from the airport. Not waste so much as an hour in Johannesburg. He'll arrive the morning after tomorrow at Jan Smuts. He can't wait to see you. That's all.'

'But Rita . . . he may miss her then?'

'I told him that. He just said plenty of time for Rita later. All he wants now is you and Gert and Springbok Spruit.' She smiled. 'Springbok Spruit includes me.'

I leaned against the kitchen table and pushed the hair back from my forehead. On the third night from now we'd be here together, my husband and I – Kobie and this newborn Jo he had long forgotten.

So soon!

❦ 18 ❦

THERE WAS THAT NIGHT IN JOHANNESBURG, MY last time alone with Rob – till that other terrible night at the lake. There were no signposts, no milestones to warn us. To us it seemed that Johannesburg was the end of the line.

May in the highveld is a perfect month. Sparkling days and frosty nights. It is early winter with the lingering tenderness of autumn to soften the edge of the wind and melt the ice that forms on quiet water.

Rob had driven north with me in my car, and the Sherards had arranged to turn in their hire-car next day at Jan Smuts airport. Kobie and Rita were due to touch down at much the same time on the following morning and the Sherards' departure was scheduled for half an hour later; so, if their respective aircraft were on time, there'd be meetings and partings all round before my husband and I set off on our homeward journey.

The Sherards spent the night with a surgeon friend in Parktown while Rob and I went to a motel not far from the airport.

We were given adjoining rooms with showers and a carport.

It was late afternoon when we signed in.

'There's a nice little bar and a very good restaurant,' said Rob. 'There's a dance floor too and taped music. What more could you ask?'

Our rooms led on to a small furnished stoep and an orange grove. Beyond it, lights twinkled on far ridges, skyscrapers stretched for the stars and the murmur of the city was like the sea at high tide. Every now and again ominous subterranean rumblings reminded us that the gold-bearing reef was honeycombed by man who had created his own vast Pluto's kingdom thousands of metres under the ground.

After we had showered and changed we sat out on that little stoep although the evening was already cold. We had never been so entirely alone.

I was half afraid. Maybe Rob was too. Tonight was loaded with the realization that this was the end. After tomorrow it was unlikely that we would ever meet again. In the past weeks my involvement had deepened into something close to worship. It was Rob who had given me back my joy in life. James Sherard had been the agent, Rob the inspiration. We had fought – and failed – to keep our relationship on a superficial plane. Now I knew beyond all doubt that I was in love with this man, but it was an alien love, altogether different from the way I felt about Kobie, who was woven into the fabric of my whole existence and being, my past and future.

'You're very serious,' Rob said. 'You still do that – escape into your own world from time to time.'

'Not very successfully. Nobody has a right to a world of their own – I've learnt that. Life is sharing.'

'Could any man share you with another?' He was smiling, but not with his eyes.

'Not my man – not Kobie.'

'I don't blame him.'

We both knew that there would be no 'sharing' tonight. Tonight I would belong solely to Rob.

Now, when I am filled with gnawing remorse for the tragedy I've brought upon all of us, I find it incredible that I was then untouched by guilt, moved only by rapture, ecstatic abandon, and sorrow that this love must end in the hour of fulfilment – here, in this little highveld motel. Parting, I believed, would be the sum total of my punishment for loving Rob. I should have known better, but I was living in a sort of transient euphoria. When you have a disability – like deafness – you often dream you're clear of it. You dream you're with people – joining in, hearing and answering; you can even dream music and the remembered call of birds. The dream had come true. I no longer woke to silence.

'They've started the band,' I said. 'Rather soothing, not too thump-thump.'

'It'll be thump-thump later. They make a distinction between dinner music and dance music. It's not a band. It's taped.'

'Have you stayed here often?'

'Twice. In transit. I never will again. Are you hungry?'

'I don't know.'

He laughed and drew me to my feet.

'Let's go and find out.'

We dined, we danced, we made love. We slept in each other's arms till my alarm-clock shrilled as the stars began to fade in the cloudless night sky. I suffocated it quickly under my pillow to let Rob sleep on a while. I lay beside him, longing to touch the thick black hair falling across his forehead, to stroke his naked shoulder and press myself against the warmth of his body. But I slipped out of bed, pulled on my warm coat and went on to the stoep that linked our rooms. Even then in the cold dawn light of the new day that would give me back to my husband I felt more trepidation than guilt. I believe now that guilt mounts slowly but surely, just as pain only follows when the numbness of a sudden severe injury wears off.

I heard a step and Rob was with me, his arms round me. He was cool, his hair damp and ruffled from his shower.

'Darling, there'll be a waiter here with our breakfast any moment. We asked for it on the stoep at seven-thirty.'

His words were practical, but his touch roused me. It was hard for us to break apart and face this difficult morning sensibly. We knew we must.

Half an hour later we were breakfasting, watching, unhurried, as the rosy sky turned to blue and sunlight filtered into the fragrant orange grove.

When Rob had set down his empty coffee cup he said:

'There must be no confessions, Jo. Confession can be a selfish sort of catharsis – you get rid of it, give yourself an undeserved absolution and leave the injured person to be tormented with a lifetime of mistrust.'

He stood leaning against the balustrade. 'Kobie's mercurial

and masterful, darling. He won't be fully prepared for the . . .
transformation . . . your new sparkle, your confidence and
outgoing attitude. All these things will come as a shock.
You'll have to make allowances – be very sensitive—'

'But surely it'll be a happy shock?'

'In a way, but you must try to see it from his angle. He's
already had to make big adjustments. It's always so when one
of two partners changes. The other changes to compensate.'

'You mean, as I got deafer, Kobie had to push me into the
things I chickened out of – meeting new people, all that. He
became the leader – the boss.'

'So right. The protector too. It's going to be bewildering
and upsetting for him to find you don't need that sort of
protection any more, to see you taking the initiative and
stealing the limelight. Quite honestly, he won't know what's
hit him, just at first.'

'Have I really changed so much?'

'You must know you have.'

'I suppose so. The whole tempo of my life and thought
has speeded up. You get sluggish when you don't hear
properly. You think, "Is that somebody calling me?" or
"Could that be the doorbell?" but you don't jump to it
because, like as not, it's nothing. You stay put in your quiet
shell – finding it more peaceful that way. Quite pleasant,
really.'

'I've been watching you throw off the lethargy – more
every day. For Kobie there's been no transition period—'

'So I must play it down – this restored vitality that throbs
right through me.'

'Let him get used to it fairly gradually.'

Rob wanted to help us along a path he feared might be more difficult than either of us could imagine.

'You frighten me. Could anything so marvellous as a miracle have side effects? Bad ones?'

He smiled down at me.

'Who knows? When the water at the wedding feast was turned to wine maybe the bridegroom got drunk as an elephant on marula berries. And how did the family of Lazarus really feel when he cast off his shroud and shook the grave dust out of his hair? Maybe his heirs weren't as delighted as they seemed.'

'You're horribly cynical.'

'A realist. In my profession we get that way.'

So, on that tingling bright morning before we went to the airport to meet Kobie – and Rita too – he tried to warn me of the quicksands ahead.

In the turmoil of Johannesburg airport we all had morning coffee together – Kobie, Rita, Rob, the Sherards and I.

Kobie's big American jet and Rita's small aircraft from Mbabane touched down within minutes of each other, and the Sherards expected to be called by Qantas at any moment. James watched Kobie with interest and he must have been gratified to notice his astonishment when I was able to take a normal part in the rather disjointed conversation. Eve could hardly keep her eyes off my beautiful sister-in-law. She couldn't know that Rita's manner towards Rob was unusually constrained and defensive.

Kobie, deeply tanned, was thinner than when he'd left this same airport only two months ago, and he'd gained in poise and authority. So he too had changed? Had there perhaps been another woman – a casual affair – somewhere along the line? Any woman could want Kobie – good to look at, physically in his prime, and always alive with high-spirited charm. It wouldn't be easy either for him to do without that side of his life. Suddenly I remembered his telephone call to me – his urgent plea when he knew the operation was a success. 'Come to me, Jo!'

It hadn't been possible then. If there had been . . . some episode . . . he'd be wondering more than ever about me, alert to emotional risks. We were in the seventh year of our marriage. Young as we were, we'd reached the first big cycle of danger in any marriage, however good. I dreaded his quickly-roused jealousy with its perceptive power. Or was I being foolish – anticipating trouble because I'd let him down?

'Passengers for Mauritius and Australia—'

The loudhailer had us on our feet to bid the Sherards goodbye. Kobie wrung James Sherard's hand.

'How can I thank you? All of us – all our family – are going to benefit from the wonderful job you've done on Jo.'

But Rita's swift glance at me was cool and speculative. What was she thinking? Presently she and Rob were standing in the sun by our car. Kobie was already at the wheel.

'Pity you can't stay for just one night.' said Rita to Kobie. 'I'm dying to hear all about your tour.'

'There's so much to do at Springbok Spruit, Ritakie. I'm sorry, but there it is. There's a big job to be tackled at home and in the Karoo. I really have had an earful and an eyeful in America. Those boys have a hell of a lot of know-how.'

He told me all about it on the long drive home through the sun-bleached highveld grasslands. I'd always heard best in a car and I guess he often forgot that at last I wasn't using any aid. No bubbles!

He, in his turn, wanted to know all about the operation and marvelled at its apparent simplicity.

'If the right man does it,' I said. 'It's very delicate – that microscopic stuff.'

In the back of my mind was a sick dread of homecoming – a growing determination that I couldn't go from Rob to Kobie so soon. In a few days perhaps. Yet I had to admit that his increased maturity was attractive and he had the same lean fitness that had always pleased me when he returned from his military training camp. Now, as he talked of the conference and all he had learned about scientific soil and water conservation, and crops for the semi-deserts of the world, I realized that he was going to follow in his father's footsteps and give life to our own dying area.

But all the time, like a cold undercurrent to our chatter, intimate excuses were forming, dissolving and re-forming deep in my mind.

Even after the day together, after the return to Springbok Spruit and the family greetings and the sundowners at which Jan Bosman and his wife joined us, we were still not used to each other – the new Jo and the new Kobie.

At last, after Christabel had put Gert to bed and the Bosmans had gone, we bathed and changed before dining up at the homestead with Ma.

'It's so strange,' said Kobie. 'You call from one room to another and hear the answers. When I was under the shower and I shouted to you, you shouted back. I can't get used to it. Stop me if I talk too loud.'

I laughed. 'You're doing that now.'

I was sitting at the dressing-table brushing my hair. He came and stroked it as if to rediscover its texture.

'You *look* the same, liefie, prettier even than I remembered. You can hear. That should bring us closer together. Why do I feel . . .' He turned away suddenly.

'Feel what?'

'As if I'd lost you?'

I swung round on the stool.

'Don't say a thing like that – just because I'm back in the world of other people!'

'Other people,' he repeated slowly. 'Yes, you don't only belong to me any more, do you?'

'Kobie, what are you getting at?'

'There were things I noticed this morning. Rita and Rob, for instance. What's gone wrong there?'

'She's making a film – as she's always hoped to do. He's going home to Australia – in August.'

'Without her?'

'That's the way she wants it.'

'She's been in Jo'burg since I left, hasn't she?'

'You *know* she has.'

'Yes,' he said. 'I know.'

'So . . .?'

'So you didn't want me to hurry home, did you? You made that very clear.'

'It would have been crazy to cut your tour short. I was with my parents—'

'Near the hospital. Near Rob.'

I got up and opened my wardrobe to get out my warm camel-hair coat.

'Ma's expecting us. We mustn't keep her waiting any longer. We're late already.'

He helped me into my coat. His arms slid round my body. I saw us reflected in the long cheval-glass, Kobie behind me, chin on my dark hair, hands crossing under the open coat, exploring as they'd so often done before, and never without my quick response. But now I didn't cover them with mine and hold them to me – tight and warm. I stood like a statue and watched my own small thin face freeze. He let me go, staring at me in the mirror, his eyes changing and questioning.

'I'm sorry, Kobie. It can't be like that tonight. Not for a few days. You understand?'

I heard my voice – brittle and cold as winter ice on the shallow pool by Gert's sandpit. I couldn't help myself. I hated and despised myself. This was my husband who had never consciously failed me in anything. But I wasn't ready yet. Too much had happened recently. I must have time – just a little time – to re-adjust.

He moved back from me as if I were a snake – carefully and quietly. He had his hunter's expression now, grim and wary-eyed, instinct taking over from reason in the face of danger.

'Yes, Jo,' he said. 'I think I understand very well.'

❧ 19 ❧

DURING THE NEXT FEW DAYS I LEARNT THAT YOU
can't wash out a love affair like a mark on the carpet. It
comes back to confront you as they say bloodstains do. But
I tried.

Our reunion, which should have been so happy, had gone
terribly wrong. The fault was mine. All the same, I couldn't
see my partner suffer without pain myself. Kobie's suffering
was my own. We knew each other with our skin, bones and
blood, with the experiences of shared childhood and of
young love awakening, with six good years of marriage,
with joy to unite us – and grief. A deaf girl and a dead baby.
As mates we had always been well suited, for my hot-
blooded husband was tender as well as passionate. Now,
suddenly, when the scrambled lines of communication
between us had been miraculously restored, we were using
them, more often than not, to wound each other.

I had forgotten that words could create misunderstandings
more easily than they ironed them out.

It was up to me to steer our marriage away from the rocks
of my own making.

Kobie was as proud as he was fiery, and after my first
rebuff he made no attempt to touch me. We lay that night

in our large double bed a thousand miles apart. The next day he said:

'Gert is nearly three. He should have his own room across the passage—'

'He has. It's his playroom.'

'He should sleep in it. There's a comfortable divan there. He's too old to be in the dressing-room any more.'

The change was made. Gert accepted it. In fact, he rather liked going to bed with all his animals and cuddly toys around him. He felt independent and important, no longer a baby next door to Mom and Pa.

Kobie had Christabel make up the dressing-room bed for himself. I wondered what she thought. She'd probably tell Annie up at the homestead that all was not well between the young *baas* and his wife and Annie would relay the information to Ma who'd be troubled.

During the days that followed, his family saw very little of Kobie. He and Jan Bosman were busy at Springbok Spruit setting various productivity pilot schemes in motion and planning the improvement of grazing for the sheep and cattle. But it wasn't only his own property that concerned him. He had come back bursting with fresh ideas for rejuvenating the waterless areas of the Karoo, and he was soon organizing farmers' meetings all over our countryside to draw up plans to save the thirstbelts from becoming dust-bowls. His ideas received wide publicity, serious attention and promises of help from interested government departments. At only twenty-four Kobie's initiative and drive had proved him a leader.

My mother-in-law and I were delighted and impressed.

As far as our intimate life was concerned, Kobie had made his protest when he'd moved Gert out of the dressing-room and himself out of my double bed. It was up to me to make the next move.

I made it a week after his return. To leave it longer would be fatal.

The night was frosty and windless. It was utterly quiet. The vast moonlit Karoo held our little home in a deep brooding spell. Waiting. Kobie had turned out his light but he was not asleep. The door between our rooms was ajar. It was seldom closed; neither of us could bear to shut the other out completely. To do that would have been to kill our marriage and maim ourselves beyond hope of recovery.

A fire crackled in my hearth and its fitful glow lent my bedroom a warm inviting human life. I stood in the doorway in my see-through nightie with my hair streaming over my shoulders, the firelight behind me flickering over my body. I well knew that in my own slight-limbed, small-breasted way I was temptation itself to Kobie. The bucolic side of my tempestuous husband was strictly for the sheep paddocks and his dairy herd. In his home he was fascinated by the delicate and the fragile; above all by the little 'dryad' he had hunted warily down the years, never roughly but with the innate understanding that is so often a quality of true simplicity. He could coax a wild bird on to his hand or win the trust of a springbok fawn. He rode his stallion with firm assurance; and, in spite of his father's fate, never hesitated to handle our fierce Friesland bull. He gentled wild creatures with infinite patience.

'Jo . . .?'

'Kobie. Isn't it time we got to know each other again?'

'Liefie – my liefie!'

So there, with the scent of the burning candlebrush and the dance of the leaping flames, we found each other once more.

After that Christabel could report to Annie that the young *baas* no longer slept in the dressing-room. My mother-in-law's face resumed its rosy serenity.

Kobie plunged into his work of beast and land redemption with greater enthusiasm than ever. His new up-to-the-minute scientific approach to a perpetual problem brought hope to many farmers who'd lived for years under the shadow of ruin.

But in trying to save our marriage from shipwreck I'd steered a drastic course right on to the hidden reef I should have guessed was there beneath the surface, more deadly than the rocks I'd tried to avoid.

One morning, at the end of July when the snow of mid-winter capped the mountains, and the aloes burned scarlet in the bush, I drove in to Verfontein with Gert. Kobie was away for a few days at various agricultural meetings throughout the Karoo.

Dr Du Toit's receptionist knew our little boy well and she had a splendid collection of toys for children in the waiting-room. Gert was absorbed with a tip-lorry and she let him squat on the floor near her desk and play with it while I went in to the doctor's consulting-room.

'Well,' he said, finally, 'I think there's no doubt about it, Jo. But if you want to be quite sure we can do the frog test.'

'Let's be quite sure.'

'Good. I'll 'phone you in a day or two and give you the result.'

He smiled and touched my ears.

'Sherard's done a great job on you. You must be very thrilled.'

'It's wonderful – being back in the world.'

When he called me on the party-line two days later to say the test was positive, I was overjoyed. I longed to tell Ma but Kobie must know before anyone else. He didn't even suspect the news I was going to tell him with such happy confidence.

He returned home in the late afternoon, weary but pleased with the beginnings that were being made. While I put Gert to bed he went up to the homestead for a drink and a chat with Ma.

'Kobie'll be tired,' she'd said to me that morning. 'Let him relax alone with you this evening. Tomorrow you can dine with me.'

I waited till we'd finished dinner and were sitting at the fireside with our coffee. Then I told Christabel to go to her room as we no longer needed her and I made sure that Gert was sound asleep. To my surprise Kobie, who seldom smoked, lit a cigarette as I rejoined him. It was one of the idiosyncrasies of my pregnancies that I disliked people smoking near me.

'Need you?' I asked. 'You didn't smoke before you went to America.'

He grinned. 'I had to go to America without you. I missed you, liefie. Smoking calmed my nerves.'

'Are you nervous now?'

'I've had a heavy few days. Anyway, you don't really object, do you? It's not a habit – just an occasional luxury. Why are you nagging me?'

I wrinkled up my nose and he laughed.

'You've never minded people smoking except when you were carrying your babies.'

'I mind now.'

I went to his chair and took the cigarette from his unresisting lips and tossed it into the fire. His eyes were wide with astonishment. I sat at his feet, my head leaning against his knee. He stroked my hair softly.

'Women have funny moods.'

'Especially when they're carrying babies.'

His hand froze on my hair. 'Wait a bit, Jo . . . What are you telling me?'

'While you were away I went to see Dr Du Toit. There's that frog test. It's positive.'

Once – not so long ago – I had been unaware of the different qualities of silence. It had been the curious negative element in which I'd learned to live. Passive. Now, since my return to the world of noise and voices, it had regained

shades and significance, from peaceful relaxed companion-
ship to a sudden cessation of sound and movement loaded
with menace. The silence following my words was so
heavily ominous that it seemed to rest on my heart and
stop it beating. I heard my own stifled cry break through
it.

'Kobie! Surely . . . surely you should be happy!'

He answered me slowly.

'There was a time when the really important decisions in
our family were taken by the two of us together. Now you
prefer to make them alone . . .' He paused. 'Or with Rob's
help.'

'Rob! What has *he* to do with this? James Sherard told
me there was very little risk. It was my own responsibility.
If the bad ear gets worse it can be dealt with later. The one
James has fixed should stay good.'

He ignored that, following his own explosive train of
thought.

'Another child . . . Isn't our family planning something
you and I ought to have discussed? We have before.'

The atmosphere in the warm cosy room was arctic.

'In the circumstances I didn't think it fair to you. You
might not have wished to let me take even the slightest
risk of my deafness recurring. It was for your sake I went
ahead without telling you. I was thinking of you and
Gert—'

'Very considerate, Jo. But what was the hurry? A companion a few months earlier or later couldn't make much
difference to Gert at his age. *What was the hurry?*'

I sprang up to face Kobie. He rose too and looked down at me steadily.

'What are you accusing me of?'

Tears of rage stung my eyes. His big hands seized my shoulders and bit into them, transmitting his resentment and suspicion.

'I'm only asking you a simple question. What was the damned hurry?'

'You came home from America—'

'And I wanted to make love to my wife – be truly back with her. You wouldn't have it—'

'That was just bad luck. Not my fault.'

'It was a woman's excuse.'

'You never accepted it, did you? That very night you turned away from me—'

'*I* did! That's rich!'

'I was afraid for our marriage after that.'

'With reason. So was I – even before that. I was afraid the moment I saw you with Rob at Jan Smuts airport. And Rob with Rita. You and he watching your steps, treading like cats on wet cement, and Rita disturbed and upset—'

'She had some excuse. She'd broken with Rob.'

'So you've told me. He was shot of her when you went to the Cape while I was away.'

I tore myself out of his grasp and sank into a chair, my face in my hands.

He crossed the room and fetched me a drink and placed it on the small table beside me.

'Kobie, you torture yourself, and me too.'

God knows, I'd earned my share of the torture. Everything that had gone wrong between us was my fault and I knew it.

I took a gulp of the brandy he'd brought me and a wave of false courage and defiance warmed my blood.

'I wanted to save our marriage,' I persisted stubbornly. 'This was my way of trying to do so. It was absolutely intentional. No accident.'

'If it was no accident there was all the more reason why it was a matter for both of us to discuss – just as your ear operation should have been.'

Explanations, recriminations; every word either of us uttered pushed us deeper into the mire.

I stared up at him, strained and despairing. He refused to believe my motive, which, at least, had been genuine.

'If you're implying that I'm deliberately attempting to force the responsibility of another man's child on to you – my husband – I must clear out for a while. . . . Think things through by myself. Such a situation . . . here . . . the two of us driving each other crazy . . . Can't you see it would be unbearable?'

My voice was shaking. I was trembling all over.

'Where do you plan to go?' he asked, cold as ice. 'To Rob Stirling?'

'Never mind where I'm going – or when!'

He watched me, trying to assess my intentions. Would I carry out my threat and leave him? Or was I like an animal demonstrating ferocity till the show-down called its bluff?

I don't believe I was sure myself till he said the one thing that could harden my purpose beyond recall and bring us to what I thought then was the end of the road.

'Go, if you must! But Gert's my son – my only child. He stays with me.'

❧ 20 ❧

THERE WAS NOTHING ORIGINAL ABOUT MY FLIGHT from home. I followed the conventional behaviour of any stupid young wife in a situation not easily resolved.

Kobie left the house as usual after an early breakfast and failed to kiss me good-bye. Once again Christabel found the dressing-room bed in confusion. The *baas* had obviously spent a restless night away from his wife. I told her to hurry with the housework and take Gert up to the *ounooi* at the homestead.

'Tell the ounooi I'll come and get him in an hour's time. If she's busy, you can play with him in the garden.'

It was a lovely bright day, cold, crisp and sunny, but I was in no mood to appreciate it.

The moment Christabel and Gert were on their way up the rise I packed for him and for me. Not very much. Three suitcases in all – enough for about a fortnight. After that we'd 'take a view', as my father would put it. I brought my car round to the front drive and put the cases in the boot and locked it. The gardener, who was dealing with a plague of ants in the backyard, was too occupied to observe the unusual happenings taking place on the other side of the house. Then I ought to have fetched Gert from the homestead. But I found that I couldn't face Ma's steady blue eyes, so I telephoned instead and asked her to send her grandson home with Christabel.

'You sound in a hurry, Jo,' she remarked.

'Yes, I'm taking Gert to Verfontein right after lunch. I have a dentist's appointment. A filling. Gert'll have to do without his rest this afternoon.'

'He'll be pleased at that!' She laughed. 'He hates his rest. Too much energy, like his father. Well, I'll see you and Kobie at dinner-time tonight. Christabel tells me she'll be baby-sitting for Gert. Kobie'll be late back, I gather.'

'Not before sunset. Totsiens, Ma.'

I hung up, feeling mean and shabby – a traitor and a liar. But my mind was made up.

When she had served our early lunch, Christabel asked me to buy a number of household necessities while I was in Verfontein. I dutifully jotted them down on a piece of paper. As soon as she turned her back I added a postscript to a note for Kobie and enclosed the list. 'We need these things. Please get them for Christabel or ask Ma to. Jo.'

There was a note of course. No beginning, no end to it. Just a statement.

'I'm taking Gert away for about two weeks.
After that I'll get in touch with you and
we can make whatever important decisions
are necessary *together*. (You see I've
learnt that lesson!) In the meantime I
must get away and think by myself. Don't

try to find me and don't worry. I'll be
all right. So will Gert. Jo.'

Gert was delighted when I bundled him into the car. Any
excuse to dodge his after-lunch nap was welcome. But he
nodded a bit in the little chair attached to the seat next to
mine.

At Verfontein I cashed a cheque at the Zebra Supermarket
and filled up with petrol. Then I stepped on it. We made
Laingsburg by nightfall. I felt worn out and quite incapable
of coping with the Cape mountain passes in the dark with a
fretful overtired child, so I took a room at the hotel. We
both needed a good night's sleep. But Gert was exhausted
and fractious. He fired endless questions at me like distress
signals. 'Where are we going, Mom?' 'Where is this place?'
'Where's Pa?' and so on – and on and on. I must have been
tense and impatient – poor little boy – because at one
moment he burst into tears, and when he finally slept with
his favourite teddy bear clasped against his chin the brown
round-eared head of the cuddly toy was damp. He wanted
Kobie and Ouma and Darkie, the spaniel, and Christabel and
the cat. He sensed that the manner of our going 'on holiday'
was all wrong. Good old instinct at work again. Right on
target.

There can be delays on our long distance country telephone exchanges but by luck I got through to Muizenberg
fairly quickly. Daddy came on the line. Though he asked
a question, he didn't sound surprised to hear my voice.

'Jo? How come you're calling from Laingsburg?'

'I'm on my way to you and Mummy with Gert. We're sleeping here tonight . . . yes, it's quite comfortable. We'll be leaving after breakfast tomorrow. Be with you before lunch.'

'I'm delighted, my girl. Mummy will be too. But what about Kobie? Should you leave him now? We've read a lot about him in the papers lately. He's doing a big job in the Karoo.'

'Don't ask me about Kobie, Daddy. I'll tell you everything tomorrow. I know he's doing a wonderful job – but we've had a sort of . . . misunderstanding. If he rings you—'

'He's already done so. He sounded frantic. You'd gone to Verfontein with Gert – and vanished. So he said.'

'I left a note. He knows we'll be all right. Please don't tell him we're on our way to you. I have to be alone for a bit – to think.'

'I promised to call him if I heard anything.'

'You mustn't, *please*. Not till I've had a chance to talk to you and Mummy. I've told him in my note that he's not to worry, that I'll get in touch with him in a couple of weeks—'

'How can he not worry? He was distraught.'

'Daddy, unless you swear to me that you won't let Kobie know where we are and where we're going, I shall take Gert somewhere else – not home to you. Somewhere even you won't know about.'

I must have sounded desperate, perhaps even hysterical. But he stuck to his point.

'I promised your husband—'

'That you'd call him when you'd heard something. Well, hold on till we turn up on your doorstep. That's all I implore you. Give me time to see you and ask your advice. If Kobie chases after us now it'll be the end. Literally. We both need time to cool off . . .'

When next he spoke I knew that my plight had touched my father. His voice came across the night and the distance and the high mountains with great clarity and understanding.

'Take it easy, Jo-Jo. Mummy and I will respect your wishes – and your judgment. We'll clam up completely till we've heard your story. God knows what it can be. I thought you and Kobie were a sound couple. Be that as it may, come to us assured of a welcome – and sympathy. If we can help you, we will.'

'Bless you, Daddy. I've never needed you more.'

'Jo . . . just one thing. Is there – for you – anybody else?'

To my horror my voice was suddenly choked with tears.

'I don't know. . . . That's one of the things I have to find out.'

'I see,' he answered gravely. 'Well, that problem must wait with any others you have to sort out. Now, go to bed and take a couple of aspirins, if you haven't anything stronger. Sleep soundly and rest assured that no one – *but no one*, except Maria – will know that you are with us till you give us the green light.'

'Thank you Daddy. You've calmed me down already. Give Mummy my love – and good night.'

I was still strung up and overwrought but the windmills thumping and whirling in my head and chest were slowing down. I went upstairs to the bathroom and was sick. That helped too.

Gert didn't stir when I undressed. He looked pale and vulnerable with his fair curls and his bear against his cheek. The bear had neither moods nor problems. He was a loved grubby extension of the child, familiar and dependable in strange surroundings where even his mother had ceased to be the source of comfort and security.

What are we doing to you, my son? I thought. What have I done to all of us?

By morning I had a grip on myself.

Gert must not be allowed to suffer because his parents had got themselves into a first-class emotional tangle.

The Matroosberg was deep in snow and we stopped the car to make snowballs and pelt each other. I was able to rejoice in his apple cheeks, sparkling eyes and fine sturdiness, in his shrieks of delighted laughter. Yet something told me that it had been folly to bring him with me. He was Kobie all over again, fusing my earliest memories with the disaster of now.

As we descended the passes to sea level the climate changed. The brilliant sun and unpolluted air of the Karoo winter gave way to the mists of the stormy Cape. The long beaches were deserted and streaked with kelp washed up by angry tides, the rollers were high with flying spray fringing a sullen heaving green ocean. The wind was damp and salty and the whole scene had the forlorn majesty of an out-of-season coast forsaken by all save the gulls wheeling against the grey sky.

'Nobody swim,' said Gert.

'It's too cold, darling.'

'Want to go home.'

But when we arrived at the flat and Maria, in purple tights and a scarlet dress, bent down to hug him and whisper in Afrikaans, 'I've made you special biscuits,' and Mummy gave him a new rubber ball with soldiers all over it, he cheered up visibly and began to adapt himself as I'd hoped he would.

Daddy went with me to garage the car. 'We've a quarter of an hour before we need appear for lunch,' he said. 'Want to stretch your legs, Jo-Jo?'

'Love it.'

We strolled along the shore and I took deep breaths of the rich ozone that was always more powerful in winter.

'Too damp after the Karoo?'

'It's another country! Gran and I used to walk miles along this beach.'

'Like your mother and I do now. Tell me, does Rob know anything about this . . . caper of yours?'

'Nothing. *He mustn't.* Do you ever see him?'

'No. There's no point in his nipping down for a quick bathe these winter days. When does he go back to Australia?'

'Next month. Second week in August.'

'So soon!'

'Anytime now.'

Daddy slipped his arm through mine and turned me towards the flat.

'Mummy'll be getting impatient. We'd better get a move on.'

Kobie telephoned the flat at nine o'clock that night. Mummy, who had answered the call, handed the receiver to Daddy.

'It's a Verfontein call. That'll be Springbok Spruit.'

I sat beside him on the stinkwood chest, scarcely daring to breathe. Here I had listened in to Kobie receiving news of his father's violent death and that shattering trans-Atlantic conversation when Kobie had disputed the wisdom of James Sherard's operating – wanting me to wait till his return. Now what?

'Is there any news for me?' he asked Daddy.

'Yes. Jo rang us up from a hotel. She made me promise not to reveal its whereabouts to anyone. She'll get in touch with you before two weeks are out. She and Gert are both well.'

'Is she . . . with Rob Stirling?'

'I assure you she is not.'

'How do you know?'

'She asked me to tell no one where she was. She particularly specified Rob.'

'When does he go back to Australia?'

'Around mid-August, I believe. That's what he told me the last time I saw him.'

'And it's the end of July now.'

I saw with a blinding flash of perception the way his mind

was working. I could read it as if he were in the hall with us. Two weeks before he could expect to hear from me. Two weeks to Rob's departure. Was I planning to leave him for Rob and abduct his son?

'Have you got Jo's telephone number?'

'She didn't give it to me.'

'I'll let it ride for ten days,' he said. 'After that I'll tear the whole damn country apart to find them.'

'Them?'

'Jo and Gert. Rob Stirling better not be with them – if he is I'll tear him apart too. Tell her that when next she rings you.'

He was talking through clenched teeth. I could see his face – his hunter's face – intent on the spoor of a dangerous wounded beast which must be destroyed. A blood spoor. A dreadful premonition invaded the little hall – a phantom form of hate and vengeance. I began to shiver.

'Kobie,' said my father, quietly. 'I suggest you give Jo the time she's asked for. I don't know what all this is about. She hasn't confided in us. No doubt she will in time – when we can all meet and unravel this tangle. It seems too complicated to handle over the telephone.'

'It certainly is, Mr Carter. This has to be thrashed out – and thrashed is the word – face to face.'

'Good night, then, Kobie. We'll keep in touch.'

Daddy hung up and looked at me thoughtfully. His face was as grey as his hair, I thought. All the summer tan gone. Or was it something else that made him look so ashen?

'You're shivering, Jo,' said Mummy. 'Come to the fire.'

I followed her and stood with my back to the electric heater. She turned on an extra bar. The damp cold was in my very marrow. Daddy lit a cigarette and I turned aside, hating the smell.

'That was a strange conversation,' he said 'But now we know which way the cat jumps.'

'But not how far. You see, I've started a baby.'

'When?' Mummy's voice was sharp.

'Two months ago – perhaps longer. Some time in May.'

'You don't look well. Does my cigarette worry you?' Daddy was always sensitive. I nodded, and he stubbed it out carefully and thoroughly. His dark eyes, so like my own, were fixed on my face as he said:

'Now, Jo, I'd be a moron if I couldn't guess what's driven Kobie up the wall. Is there any justification for thinking this child might be Rob's?'

'Of course not! Unless . . .'

'Unless what?' Mummy needle-keen again.

'Unless the pill is . . . not . . . infallible.'

She stared at me and I saw her expression harden. She was the teacher who had caught out a pupil in some abominable act. Pulling the wings off a fly, baiting an animal, drawing a filthy picture – or worse.

'You! So you're no better than any of your so-called permissive generation.'

'I've let you down – worse than Kobie. You brought me up and taught me right from wrong. He only married me—'

'Jo, be quiet! Mary, we're not sitting in judgment on our

daughter. We're out to help her. You can't assess her temptations but at least we can consider the possible result like civilized beings.'

'Daddy,' I said, in love and gratitude. 'I wanted to give Kobie another child. When he came back from America our marriage seemed to shake – like an earth tremor, a sort of warning. I wanted to shore it up, make it safe again. All right, then, I did have . . . a sort of affair . . . with Rob. It all came out of my hearing again. Through him I'd got back my youth, my joy in life. I loved him for it—'

'You don't have to explain. I've no difficulty understanding—'

Mummy stared at him as if she'd never really seen him before. Her mouth was thin and bitter.

'So you tried to make amends,' Daddy went on. 'But the timing was bad.'

'Perhaps it was – but till this minute I never doubted this child was Kobie's. With him I took no precautions.'

'With Rob you did?'

'Of course. Anyway, it was all over with Rob before Kobie got back.'

'Does Rob know about your condition?'

'No, and he never will from me. We don't write. It was good-bye in Johannesburg. Finished, done with.'

But the words were daggers. Rob was part of me now – the voice of a man, the cry of a child, the song of a bird, the rustle of leaves and the thunder of surf. He was a step in a hospital corridor, recognized though hitherto unheard.

And Kobie knew as much, because he too was part of me.

❧ 21 ❧

THE WEEK THAT FOLLOWED WAS STORMY, WITHIN and without. My mother didn't attempt to hide her disapproval and disappointment where I was concerned, though with Gert she was always sweet. It was Daddy who realized how closely I'd associated the blessing of my restored hearing with Rob, and the way it had brought us together, adding a new dimension to the attraction we'd always felt for each other.

'If it hadn't been for Rob – for his minding about me enough to insist, regardless of Kobie's opposition – I would have gone on funking surgery. He sold me James Sherard, he made me snatch at that lifeline. And it *was* a lifeline, Daddy . . . a miracle to me.'

'I know. I'd watched – with great distress – as you gradually retreated more and more into your own world, and I've also watched you make your marvellous come-back. I believe that, with patience, Kobie could be persuaded to understand how your . . . miracle, as you put it, turned into a boomerang.'

We were walking along the beach together as we so often did, leaving Gert in the Children's playground under Mummy's supervision. He adored the swings and slides.

'The fact that Rob has neither written to you nor seen you – that he doesn't even know you're here – and that he'll be back in Australia any day now, makes it easier.'

'Easier?'

'For you and Kobie to reach a reconciliation.'

'I can't live with Kobie if he's going to go on hating me.'

'He's jealous – with reason – and quick-tempered but he's not vindictive—'

'I don't know. That's never yet been put to the test.'

'When this baby is born he'll see that it's his. I'm sure of that.'

When I was with my father I felt more hopeful – as if, after all, our marriage, like my hearing problem, could 'come good'.

Whenever Kobie rang the flat, as he frequently did, Daddy gave him encouraging news of us but never betrayed our whereabouts. He let Kobie assume that I telephoned my parents regularly from my secret hide-out.

'I have the impression,' Daddy said, 'that this time for reflection is as necessary to him as it is to you.'

We were so close, Daddy and I, in those days of inner turmoil for me. Once, when we were alone, I said:

'Did things ever go wrong between you and Mummy? I feel there must have been something once to make you understand me the way you do.'

He spread his hands with a gesture that was like a shrug – I noticed how like my own hands they were, thin-fingered and expressive – and he said with a half smile that was both disillusioned and philosophical:

'My girl, your mother and I celebrate our silver wedding next year. That's twenty-five years, quarter of a century! Fundamentally, ours is a happy and splendid marriage – as yours has been and can be again – but I don't deny there've been stormy passages. The early period of most marriages is an unconscious fight for supremacy – a battlefield till the truce is declared and the compromise safely achieved – not without wounds on both sides. And wounds leave scars.'

'I'm beginning to guess. You were away fairly often – buying for Zebra . . .'

My father must have been attractive to women with his black hair and melting eyes and that air of humorous chivalry. He reflected the mischief in my eyes now, and laughed.

'Oh, yes, I know all about temptation, Jo-Jo. But your mother had holidays too – here with Gran.'

'Mummy has the faults of her virtues. She's rigid and self-disciplined. You wouldn't have to worry.'

'She's been young too—'

'She's forgotten. You haven't.'

'Some things are never forgotten. They can only be forgiven. It hurts her to see you make the sort of mistake I was liable to make. And she doesn't like to see me appear to condone it. In a way, she's on Kobie's side. We love him, you know. He too has the faults of his virtues – he's a hot-blooded man. A real man. He's also cursed with a vivid imagination.'

'Can one love . . . be in love with . . . two people at the same time?'

'I'd say yes to that – in theory. But the two people

concerned seldom accept such a situation without a great deal of anguish. It can be done in certain cases. The *ménage à trois* is a commonplace. But more often the eternal triangle ends in renunciation on somebody's part. Or tragedy.'

'You have all the answers.'

'I'm over fifty,' said my father. 'More than twice your husband's age.'

Our ninth day at Muizenburg dawned like any other – except that it was so very beautiful, one of those shining days that interrupt the Cape winter, anticipating spring. The clouds were few and dazzling white, the sea blue as the sky, glittering with life and movement. The first arums glimmered round the *vleis*, the oaks in the valleys showed young leaf as they do in August, and the woods and mountains called.

'It's ideal for a picnic,' said Mummy. 'Let's give Maria the day off and go to Tokai – the pine forests.'

So we did that.

Now, when I think of that day, it has a strange elusive quality. It was the calm before the storm. By some curious alchemy of light and pine-scented air, it melted away the dross of guilt, remorse and apprehension that rested so heavily upon my heart since our flight from Springbok Spruit. It was a day set apart. Mummy, who was always at her best with her grandson, included me in her benign mood and allowed me to forget that I was her black sheep. Daddy was tranquil and amusing; he enjoyed grilling chops and sausages on our old picnic *braai*. Gert had, in his adaptable fashion, settled down once more in the well-known Muizenberg flat; he chuckled and laughed and enjoyed himself enormously. After we had eaten, Daddy gave him a little lesson.

'Now, my boy, you're nearly three and there is something everybody has to know. Never, never, never do you go away and leave a fire that has one spark of life in it. Or the wind could fan it and the forest be burned. Watch me! I pour water on the ashes, then, to be doubly sure, I cover them with earth.'

Gert helped. To be invited to play with fire and water – what bliss! Mummy gave him a basket, and, while we rested under the trees, he ran around filling it with fir cones.

'We'll give them to Maria,' Mummy said. 'She has a friend who has a real fireplace in her house. Not an electric heater like ours in the flat. Fir cones make a pretty fire. Lovely colours.'

'We have a fireplace at home,' said Gert.

I thought of Springbok Spruit and our candlebrush fires, and Kobie, and that last awful night. But in a queer detached almost painless way. Today was special, blessed with peace. I yielded to the joy of listening to sounds that so short a time ago were dead to me. Doves cooing in the branches; a pair of squirrels almost flying as they chased each other from one bough to the next; the thud of hooves as a young girl cantered her Palamino along a firepath. Girl and horse had the same blonde manes and look of breeding. Some way off a boy was playing a guitar and a puppy ran round in circles barking and trying to catch his own tail. A breeze sighed through the pine needles and a bokmakierie called to his mate with ringing melodious notes.

'They think it's spring,' said Mummy. 'Such pretty birds, green and yellow and black velvet.'

'It feels like spring.'

For me too the whole essence of nature's mating-season seemed trapped in that one shining premature spring day.

We drove home before the long evening shadows chilled the air.

As Daddy drew up we saw a familiar car parked outside the flats and a long-limbed figure standing beside it, plugging a small pipe. As Rob looked up the breeze caught his shock of black hair. It was damp and unruly. He'd been swimming.

My heart stood still. I held Gert more tightly against me as if his warm little body could somehow fill the awful arid emptiness that suddenly made a desert of my soul. As Rob stood transfixed I knew only too well why he had come.

Tomorrow morning the Springbok flight to Australia left Johannesburg.

After today I would never see him again.

As we entered the flat Rob said:

'It was such a gorgeous day I had to have one last swim – a good tide and wonderful surfing. Then I came here but got no answer to the doorbell—'

'Maria's out,' said Mummy, rather distant.

He smiled as if he didn't notice her cool attitude. 'I guessed that, Mrs Carter. So I thought I'd wait. You see, I fly home tomorrow – for good – and I couldn't go without saying good-bye to you both.'

He turned to me. 'But Jo, I'd no idea you were here. When did you come?'

'Just over a week ago.'

He looked stunned. 'And you didn't ring me or let me know . . .'

Daddy cut in. 'You'll have a sundowner, Rob. What shall it be?'

'A beer, Mr Carter, if you have it.'

'Of course. What time do you take off?'

'The early flight tomorrow – seven a.m. – I have to connect with South African Airways in Johannesburg.'

'It's a long flight to Sydney,' said Mummy, making conversation, still in her remote voice.

'I'm breaking the journey at Perth to spend a few days with my sister and her family at Sun Downs.'

'Jennie and Jack! Give them my love, Rob. The little girls'll be quite big now. Let's see, Dimples'll be seven and Anna six. When we were there with all of you I'd just started Gert and he's already rising three.'

Yes, at Sun Downs I'd been about as far gone with Gert as I was now with this baby who'd been intended to cement a quaking marriage – the baby my husband believed to be Rob's.

'Jo,' said Rob. 'I'm not dressed for taking a saucy girl out to dinner, but we could go somewhere quite informal like the Krazy Kat Klub on Zeekoevlei. Why not come with me? Goodness knows when we'll meet again—'

'If ever!' I made myself say it flippantly.

My mother was looking at me, silently warning me to refuse. I ignored her and didn't even glance at Daddy who was helping himself to a Scotch and soda.

'Well, why not?' Rob urged.

I could hear Maria, who had just come in, pottering in the kitchen getting the evening meal. My parents had a couple coming in for a game of bridge. I wanted, above all things, to go with Rob – to be alone with him just once more.

'Would you mind, Mummy?' I said at last. 'You've got the Macdonalds later, and I'll put Gert to bed before we go.'

'You must do as you think right.' Her face was carefully expressionless. I saw Rob stiffen, his eyes narrow and bright.

I said: 'I'd love to dine with you, Rob. It doesn't matter what we wear at the Krazy Kat. Anything goes. I'll just put Gert to bed, clean myself up a bit and I'll be all set.'

Gert wailed at the suggestion of bed so soon.

'Leave him to me,' said Mummy firmly. 'And Maria will give him his supper. You two go and enjoy yourselves.'

But her eyes were icy and her manner implied that the sooner we were out of the flat the better she'd be pleased. For her the lovely day was ended. My lover was making his last claim and meeting no resistance. I sensed that my father saw it differently, with greater sympathy, but with misgivings too.

When I went to my room to change and tidy up, Gert

was showing Rob his tiny toy cars and aeroplanes and miming their performance with noises to match.

There was a knock on my door and Daddy came in. I was nearly ready.

'My girl, this . . . date . . . is unfortunate.'

'It's fate, Daddy. It wasn't planned. You know that.'

He sat on the edge of my bed as I put the finishing touches to my hair and eyelashes. I was wearing trim warm slacks and a turtle-necked lime green sweater that added a brilliance to my eyes – or perhaps it was there anyway that evening.

'I know it wasn't planned, Jo. In fact, I've never seen two people look more shaken than you did when you saw each other.' He paused before he added: 'Would you resent a piece of fatherly advice—?'

In the mirror I could see my face set obstinately.

'I'm going to the Krazy Kat with Rob – if that's what you hope to stop.'

'I know that. I want to ask you a question. It's important.'

I slung my long-strapped bag across my shoulder and picked up my duffel-coat.

'Well, Daddy?'

'Do you propose to tell Rob—?'

'That I'm going to have a baby?' I smiled. 'Not unless he lights that pipe again. Thank goodness he knocked it out before we came into the flat!'

Daddy rose. 'I'm glad. This is hard for you, Jo. But it has to be this way. Come back early. Tonight must be the end of this chapter in your life. Kobie has suffered enough.'

§ 22 §

THE KRAZY KAT KLUB WAS LICENSED FOR WINES BUT not for hard liquor, so Rob ordered a bottle of Cabernet from Heracles, the Greek head-waiter.

'Just warm it a bit,' he said, 'and bring us two dry sherries and the menu.'

'Of course, Dr Stirling. It's nice to welcome you and Madame again. The winter's a dull season for us.'

'A rest from your busy summer,' smiled Rob. 'Looks as if we have the place to ourselves.'

'So far, yes. But sometimes, on a beautiful night like this, other people – like yourselves – turn up.'

We chose a corner table by the big landscape window. In summer the patio outside was lit with Japanese lanterns and couples danced there. It was a favourite haunt of ours and our friends. A well kept-lawn led down to the glimmering waters of the lake, fenced by nature with clumps of bulrushes and bamboo thickets beloved of the birds. Last summer a colony of flamingoes had settled here and their rosewinged flight at sunset had been breathtaking.

The room was warmed by a blazing log-fire in an open hearth – 'You could roast a sheep in there,' said Rob – and the crackle of the flames was accompanied by soft taped music in the background. Beyond the quiet water, a swollen blood-red moon rose above the eastern mountains.

Heracles brought a bottle of dry sherry and set it on our table with two glasses and a small platter of thin wafery biscuits and cheese snacks.

'I suggest a mixed grill with salad,' he said. 'We have delicious lamb chops and kidneys – Karoo lamb, the best in the world—'

'Ah, now, I'm going back to wonderful sheep country tomorrow—'

'To Australia, sir? We'll be very sorry to lose you.'

'I'm sad to leave South Africa.'

Heracles turned away to relay our order to the bearded hippie behind the grill with his tall jaunty chef's cap and big white apron. I looked into Rob's eyes with sad disbelief.

'I can't take it in – that you're going . . . within hours . . .'

'Nor can I. But it's better so. There has to be a final break. There's no middle road for you and me. Jo, why didn't you let me know you were here at the Cape?'

'Because – like you – I realize that there isn't a middle road for us.'

'Fair enough. But I simply can't understand why you should bring Gert to the Cape just now. Kobie hasn't been back from America all that long and he certainly can't join you. He's doing a fine job in his area from all accounts. He'll be a really big name in agriculture one day soon – if he isn't already. You usually only come to the sea in summer. So why *now*?'

I longed to tell him – to spill it all out. Everything. When

Heracles appeared at our table with the mulled red wine *en carafe*, and removed the sherry and snacks, I was grateful for the interruption. He brought the wooden bowl of tossed salad and our grills, as smoky and appetizing as the *braaivleis* Daddy had cooked in the pine forests earlier this same day. Daddy's words came back to me. 'Tonight must be the end of this chapter in your life . . .'

But Rob didn't let it alone.

'I have to know what's happened, darling.'

I pushed the tender meat around on my plate and made a pretence of eating. The red wine warmed my throat and cheeks.

'Kobie and I had a sort of row – a quarrel —'

'About us . . . you and me?'

I nodded. 'He guessed. I felt I must get away for a bit and let us both cool off.'

'Does he know where you are?'

'No. I wouldn't let Daddy and Mummy tell him. In a day or two I will. After you've gone. He rings them up at the flat and Daddy answers, but he gives nothing away – just reassures Kobie that he's heard from me – that Gert and I are all right.'

'I knew it would be difficult for Kobie and you – the altered balance of power. But I thought he'd be so glad and thankful for your sake—'

'He is! Oh, Rob, he is! Ma, too. They're all so thrilled that I'm not deaf any more. Kobie has never wanted power over me at the price of my hearing. That . . . dominance . . . was forced on him when I kept backing out of things.'

'But he doesn't like to think that now – because I inter-vened – *I* may have gained a certain protective power. Is that it?'

'I guess it is. Come, let's dance, darling. There's so little time left . . . so little . . .'

Heracles turned the tape up and the lights down as we took the floor. Rob held me closely. I wondered if he noticed that my waist had thickened slightly and my bosom was fuller. I was vaguely aware of Heracles clearing our table and of another young couple coming in through the arched doorway and being placed near the fire away from our window. I felt that I could dance with Rob for ever. But the tape changed to one we didn't like, so we stopped and walked back to our table. His hand was lightly on my arm. It was as if we couldn't bear to lose physical contact with each other. I wonder now if that was written on our faces. I was absorbed in Rob, moving in a trance, lost to my surroundings, to anyone else.

Suddenly, as we passed the door to reach our table, I felt his fingers tighten on my arm. It was like being wakened from a dream.

The tall fair-haired figure standing so still in the archway moved forward.

'Mind if I join you?' said Kobie, voice and eyes hard as steel.

From that instant there wasn't the slightest doubt that this was the showdown.

Kobie drew a chair up to our table and sat down with us.

He took his brandy flask from the pocket of his sheepskin jerkin and poured a stiff tot into Rob's unused goblet intended for iced water. I passed the jug in silence. He shook his head.

'You don't usually take your brandy neat,' I said.

'I don't usually find my wife about to leave me for my sister's lover.'

'Kobie, you're drunk or crazy!' Rob filled my glass and his own with wine as he spoke.

'Am I?' Kobie took a swig of brandy and set down his goblet with deliberation. He was neither drunk nor crazy. He had followed a spoor to the end and I knew that it was Rob who was at bay.

'Listen, then! This is what happened. Let me give you the sequence.'

Kobie leaned forward, his eyes fixed relentlessly on Rob.

'I come home from America. My wife doesn't want to know about me for the first week. Then she thinks better of it. I'm taken in.' He smiled bitterly. 'Yes, in every sense of the word. A little over two months later she announces that she's pregnant. She – who doesn't make mistakes when it comes to having babies, because she daren't – has got into this condition without my knowledge or agreement—'

'Jo! Is this true?'

'You needn't put on the astonished act, Rob Stirling. You know it's true.'

'He doesn't know anything of the sort!' I cut in sharply. 'I haven't told him.'

Kobie ignored me, his face hard as granite.

'Jo and I have an argument – so bitter that she takes off and leaves me the next day. She simply disappears with our son. There's a note telling me not to try to find her or get in touch with her. I telephone her parents. They deny all knowledge of her whereabouts. I ring them constantly and they assure me that Jo and Gert are well and safe, but refuse to give me her address or telephone number. I must leave her alone for a fortnight. Then she'll contact me. *Her* rules for playing this game, you notice, *her* ultimatum. Or perhaps *yours*—'

'Kobie! You're misinterpreting everything—'

'Be quiet, Jo!'

His quick glance at me was blazing, then he turned back to Rob, who watched him white-faced and tight-lipped.

'This morning the cat jumps out of the bag. Till then I've telephoned in the evenings after a hard day's work. This morning is the tenth day since Jo left Springbok Spruit with Gert. I make up my mind to wait no longer. I'll give her parents one more chance to tell me where she is. If they refuse, I'll get detectives on to the job. So I ring the Muizenberg flat at midday. Maria answers. I tell her I want to speak to Mr or Mrs Carter. This is her answer. "They've all gone out for a picnic. They left half an hour ago." *All*? I say. She gasps and hangs up on me.'

Poor Maria, I thought. Such a silly slip!

'Within the hour I'm on my way.'

Not drunk, not crazy, but by nightfall, in the Cape mountains, he'd have taken a benzedrine tablet as he'd often done on long lonely drives when he was afraid of falling asleep at the wheel. Probably no food. Then a strong brandy. Or two – or more. I'd noticed that his flask had been half empty. As if my thoughts sparked off the idea in him, he poured another double tot into his glass.

'I arrive at the flat – perhaps an hour ago . . . less, I should think. Jo's parents are still up. They'd had a couple in to bridge with them. Mr Carter tries to play it cool, but Jo's mother comes clean because I say, "Where's Gert? I know he's here." And before she can bite her tongue, she says, "Don't wake him. He's had a long day." "I'll wake him, and he'll talk," I say "I've come to find Jo and nothing on God's earth will stop me." So there it is. Mr Carter looks reproachful when his wife tells me Jo's gone to the Krazy Kat with Rob. She adds, by way of excuse, that Rob flies home tomorrow. And every instinct in me shrieks that Jo means to fly with him. That's why she doesn't want to speak to me or see me. Nothing must come between her and her intention. But it does, you see. I find her – and I'll stop her!'

He rose with clenched fists and jaw taut.

'Kobie, sit down!' Rob was on his feet too, aware of the menace in Kobie's attitude. 'We have to talk this out—'

'We have to fight it out. I'm going to beat hell out of you!'

Rob had his back to the plate glass window, and, as Kobie lunged towards him, he put up his guard. I'd seen Kobie box many times from boyhood into manhood, I'd seen him belligerent and pugnacious, out for blood, but never before had I seen stark murder in his face. Rob saw it too and he was quick. He got in the first blow, a body blow over the heart, but Kobie came back at him with a thundering left to the jaw that threw his head back. Rob's eyes glazed and he reeled as Kobie's right crashed into the side of his temple, knocking him against the heavy glass pane. Blood gushed from his nose and mouth as he fell.

'Get up and fight!' Kobie bent over him to drag him to his feet.

'Stop!' I cried. 'You'll kill him! For God's sake, stop!'

I doubt if Kobie heard me. He was seeing red and nothing could hold him any more. All the brooding and pent up anguish of many weeks, all his sense of betrayal was concentrated at this moment in his vengeful fists. I looked wildly round me and seized on the only weapon that came to hand – the near empty wine bottle on our table. I grabbed it and brought it crashing down on the back of my husband's head. I heard the sickening thud as I struck him a second time. I heard something else – my own dry sobbing.

Kobie spun round dizzily. He glared at me in total disbelief before he collapsed against the table and slowly buckled, blood and wine matting his bright hair where the bottle had gashed his skull.

I was vaguely aware of the commotion all round me – the young couple by the fire rushing across the floor; the hippie chef in his high starched cap supporting me, his gentle bearded face strangely Christ-like; Heracles stooping over Kobie, feeling for a heartbeat, the music going on and on – an old outdated favourite, 'This is my lovely day'.

'Mrs Van der Walt, are you all right?'

He was saying it again and again. I looked into his anxious dark eyes, his cap was crumpled, his arm kept me from slipping off the chair into which he had lowered me. I was dazed, and deep in my body there was pain.

'I killed him,' I said to the chef. 'I've killed my own husband.'

A nurse was holding my wrist. I was vaguely aware of contrivances attached to my limbs. Drips, tubes into my veins anchored by Elastoplast.

'Where am I?'

'You're in Groote Schuur Hospital.'

'My baby . . . has my baby miscarried?'

Her fingers pressed against my pulse.

'It's all right so far. But you must keep very quiet – not move or get agitated—'

'Rob . . . I want to see Dr Stirling.'

Her voice became expressionless. 'Dr Stirling is not available. I'm going to give you an injection, Mrs Van der Walt.'

I had a tiny room to myself. Through the window I could see Devil's Peak flooded with rose.

'Is it sunrise?' I asked the nurse, as she prepared the syringe.

'Sunset.'

She swabbed my arm with something cold. The prick of a needle. It was night.

Full sunlight poured into the little room. A young nurse was smiling down at me, not the one who had said, 'Dr Stirling is not available.'

Appalling memories began to revive in the light of the new day. Blows, blood, Rob smashed against plate glass, Kobie's bright head gashed and bleeding, the sorrowful eyes of the hippie chef . . .

'How long have I been here?'

'You were brought in very early yesterday morning – about two o'clock.'

'What day is it?'

'Saturday.'

Saturday? And the Australian jet left Johannesburg on Friday. Yesterday.

'Rob . . .' I said weakly. 'Has Dr Stirling—'

She popped a thermometer into my mouth, held my wrist and studied her watch.

'There,' she said when she'd written something on a chart. 'Now I'm going to fetch you some tea and a little dry toast.'

Her short skirt whisked round the corner of the door. I heard a man's step and her voice outside in the corridor.

'She seems quite with it this morning, Doctor. Beginning to ask questions. She's asking about Dr Stirling—'

'The bleeding?' A man's deep voice broke in abruptly, choking her off.

'Not much now.'

'Good. I'll go in.'

Dr Rabinowitz, the gynaecologist in charge of my case, was very dark and stocky with longish hair, a blue chin and searching black eyes. When he'd completed his examination he sat in the one easy chair in the little room and waited for me to speak. He seemed relaxed, which helped.

'Doctor, can you save my baby?'

'If it's humanly possible – and with your co-operation – we'll prevent a miscarriage. Now, tell me, can you recall the circumstances under which you were brought here?'

I shook my head. 'Not in any detail. Only the fight and hitting Kobie – my husband – that ghastly blow.' I covered my face with my hands to shut that out.

'Take it easy, Mrs Van der Walt!'

'If only I could talk to Dr Stirling it would help. Or has he gone to Australia already?'

'Dr Stirling has gone. I'm sorry.'

The room began to swim . . . red shot with black . . . Black. Sensation ebbing from fingers and toes.

'Sister!'

When Mummy came in the afternoon, leaving Daddy to entertain Gert, I asked no questions and answered none. I was terrified of what I might learn. I lay with closed eyes, pretending to be doped. Or perhaps I was.

For three days only my parents were allowed to see me. If anybody tried to tell me or ask me anything about the night I was brought to Groote Schuur I blacked out. Every time. They gave up.

Then Rita came.

I woke from my afternoon rest to see her sitting in the

armchair. A shaft of sunlight gilded her hair. I knew she'd been watching me, willing me to open my eyes. Her own were not sky blue, as I had always thought, but ice blue. She rose and stood over me. I felt her enmity. No use to black out now. No escape.

'What are you doing here, Rita? I thought you were in Johannesburg . . . and I'm not allowed visitors.'

'You're going to have plenty very soon. The police are waiting for the green light.'

'The police!'

'That's what I said. I gather from your mother that you're not talking and you're not listening. Well, perhaps you can read. I'll leave these with you – the front page of the *Rand Daily Mail* and cuttings from the *Cape Times* and *Argus* the day after . . . the tragedy. They may stimulate your dormant memory.'

She took the clippings from her bag and put them on the white coverlet close to my hand. Then she turned on her heel without another word. I found myself alone.

The drips had gone and my hands were free. I picked up the front page of the *Rand Daily Mail* and the banner headlines met my eyes and exploded in my brain.

WELL-KNOWN KAROO FARMER KILLS SURGEON

Jakobus van der Walt, who recently made headlines with his enterprising endeavours to improve farming prospects in the Karoo, arrived unexpectedly in the Cape Peninsula late on Thursday night to spend a holiday at the Muizenberg home of his wife's parents, Mr and Mrs Joseph

Carter. He found that his attractive young wife, Josephine, had gone out with Dr Robert Stirling of Groote Schuur Hospital and Sydney, Australia. He followed the couple to the lakeside Krazy Kat Klub where he challenged Stirling to a fight, in the course of which Van der Walt struck Stirling a blow on the temple causing brain haemorrhage resulting in death. Meanwhile Josephine van der Walt had seized a wine bottle and crashed it against her husband's head, apparently in a vain attempt to save her alleged lover from a fatal assault. Van der Walt was taken to Groote Schuur Hospital suffering from a fractured skull. His wife lies in another ward in the same hospital with a threatened miscarriage.

The cutting fell from my numb fingers.

'Dr Stirling is not available. . . .' 'Dr Stirling has gone. . . .' No good blacking out any more. The cold presence of truth had entered the room.

The new figure stood at my bedside looking down at me with clear dispassionate green eyes. She picked up the cutting that lay on the white coverlet.

'Who gave you this?'

'My sister-in-law. Rita van der Walt.'

'When?'

'Just before you came in.'

'You've read it?'

'Yes.'

'Then it's no use blacking-out any more to avoid the truth.'

'Who *are* you?'

'I'm your psychiatrist, Dr Elizabeth Kidston. Dr Rabinowitz thinks I can help you. Truth is sometimes very difficult to face alone. You need an experienced ally.'

'Are you my ally?'

'Yes,' she said. 'Ask me what you want to know.'

'Is it true? Is Rob . . . dead?'

'It's true.' Those two words confirmed the fact I had known all along and refused to accept. Even then I couldn't *feel* that it was true – I felt only emptiness.

'And Kobie?' I said at last.

'His surgeon expects him to make a full recovery—'

'To face a murder charge?'

'I suppose that's possible. I don't know.'

'It's I who should face that charge! Everything is my fault. Everything! It's strange but, after I could hear again, I've felt quicker on the draw all round. You see, my deafness induced a lethargy that soft-pedalled my whole attitude to life. When that lifted I changed—'

As I paused, she said, 'You became more forceful, more positive – returned to normal, in fact.'

'Normal? Is a normal person aggressive?'

'At times. Under provocation.'

'I couldn't have struck at Kobie like that . . . before. No matter what the provocation . . .' I covered my face with my hands.

'We'll go into all that later,' she said quietly. 'Now I want you to rest. The blacking-out phase is over. When you wake we'll face whatever is to come.'

She gave me a capsule of some sort and a glass of water. 'Swallow this, Mrs Van der Walt. You'll sleep without dreaming and you'll wake without confusion. Then we'll talk again.'

Liz Kidston stayed with me till I fell asleep.

❧ 23 ❧

WHILE DR RABINOWITZ WAS BATTLING TO SAVE MY baby Kobie was undergoing surgery for a fractured skull. My doing! A long anxious period of unconsciousness followed, and, when at last this lifted, it was considered inadvisable for me to see him. I pleaded with Dr Rabinowitz.

'I could be taken into the ward on one of those trolleys.'

'Yes,' he agreed, 'but we're thinking as much of your husband as of you.'

'Does he know what he's done? About Rob? And what I did – that I bashed him the way I did?'

'Mrs Van der Walt, these things have to filter through gradually. A man isn't in a deep coma one instant and fully with it the next. We're all aware of the emotional as well as the physical aspects of his case – and yours. When he asks for you, I assure you—'

'*If* he asks for me, you mean. He may not. It's I who am doing the asking.'

But there were plenty of other people doing plenty of asking as Rita had warned me there would be.

Dr Rabinowitz and Dr Elizabeth Kidston kept the police interrogations as short as they could. I was not to be unduly distressed. My father was always with me when I was questioned and so was his lawyer, Mr Denny, a dry little man with a face like crumpled parchment illumined by small gleaming beetle-black eyes. I told Major Van Heerden, my interrogator, the truth and nothing but the truth. But as for the *whole* truth? How absurd! The whole truth can never be condensed into a matter of hours or compressed into the space of a hospital ward or a witness box.

Ma had come to Cape Town with Rita to be near Kobie while his life hung in the balance. One day, about a week after he had regained consciousness, Liz Kidston said:

'Your mother-in-law would like to see you for a few minutes. Can you take it?'

'Yes.'

She came in – the tall golden mother of Kobie and Rita – still erect, but gaunt and greying, as if the wings of death had brushed her too. The vivid blue eyes that looked down upon me were austere, but strangely without reproach. She did not sit down.

'It was all my fault – everything,' I said. 'I don't ask you to try to forgive me.'

'You had your problem,' she answered. 'And Kobie had his temperament. Nothing is entirely one person's fault. Nothing is simple.'

I felt the tears sting my eyes.

'Will Kobie see me?'

She shook her head.

'Why not?'

'He knows what has happened. When he is better he will be charged with murder.'

I shuddered. 'He blames me?'

She brushed that aside. 'It's wiser that you don't meet till after the verdict. That's the way he wants it. He sent you a message. This time the decision is his, he says, and it is *he* who makes the rules.' A wan half-smile touched her lips. 'You see, he hasn't changed all that much.'

'Tell him I understand. When he wants to see me I'll be waiting. It's up to him.'

She didn't come again. Rita did though. She asked nobody's permission. Just appeared as she had done before, with the same frozen look in her eyes. It was late afternoon. My parents had come and gone.

'Why are you here when you hate me so much?' I asked her.

'There are things you ought to know.'

'Such as . . .?'

'Rob's ashes. Yesterday a Qantas pilot – a friend of his – flew them to Perth. His sister, Jennie, will scatter them on Sun Downs.'

I must have gone pale and pinched, for she said bitterly:

'That shakes you. Sun Downs was where you first coiled yourself round his heart like a little black snake. You – with your haunted eyes and lovely face – were so unsure of yourself you had to catch a man to make you feel attractive – to convince you that your deafness didn't matter. You did better. You turned your disability into a bond between you—'

'Rita! Don't say these things! Rob was your lover long before —'

'Before he was yours. Maybe technically that's true. But, in fact, you were always there on the sideline – the little dark, disturbing shadow, the coveted wife of another man, a strong, dominating man ready to kill any rival who tried to take you from him.' She came close to my bed, lips curled back in contempt. 'You did a great job on two fine men – the killer and the slain.'

I turned my head away on the pillow, but her icy fury had the power to burn into my brain. She wasn't acting this time.

'Tomorrow,' she said, 'I'm taking Kobie from this hospital to the Magistrate's Court where he'll be charged with murder.'

The procedure was brief. Jakobus van der Walt was charged with the murder of Robert Stirling. No evidence was led and he was released on bail pending a summary trial in the Supreme Court early in November.

Daddy explained to me that the 'summary' trial, ordered by the Attorney General, dispensed with the formality of a full preparatory examination in the Magistrate's Court.

'So now Kobie can return to his job until he has to come to Cape Town for the trial. Mrs Van der Walt went back to Springbok Spruit a few days ago and Rita set off with Kobie directly after the proceedings this morning.'

'Is he well enough to go home?'

'I suppose so, Jo. He's been discharged from hospital. And today Dr Rabinowitz told me that we can fetch you next week – that is if we can guarantee to keep you very quiet. No excitement. No exertion. Cotton-wool living, my girl.'

When Liz Kidston bade me good-bye the following week she said:

'What about your note books? I want you to carry on with the A to Z therapy.'

'Z . . .? Oh, Liz, I'm so scared.'

'If your husband had failed to recover,' she said bleakly, '*you* would have been the one to face a trial. Go on facing facts instead, Jo. You're building up courage as well as self-knowledge. You've shown that here. You've held on to this baby with great fortitude and faith —'

'Faith?' The word surprised me.

'I believe so.'

'I had faith once . . . that this baby could save our marriage and make the future come good. But now . . .'

'An act of faith reaps a reward,' she said. And added: 'I'll come and see you at Muizenberg.'

'Please do, Liz. I'm going to need your help . . . especially in November.'

When Daddy took me to the flat, Gert was waiting eagerly with Mummy. He flung himself at me as we came through the door and had to be told that, because of his unborn brother – or sister – I couldn't pick him up or let him spring into my lap or play any but the quietest games with him. He was full of questions. Where was Pa? Why didn't Rob come to see us any more? He was disturbed as he had been when we'd fled from Springbok Spruit.

'He'll adapt himself,' said Mummy. 'He's very buoyant. But sensitive to atmosphere. We must all be as calm and normal and cheerful as possible.'

I smiled, recognizing the technique.

'I get the message, Mummy.'

One morning Kobie's counsel came to see me. Advocate Bernstein was a little fair man with quick pale eyes behind strong spectacles, close lips and a long narrow nose that twitched when he was on the scent of something to his client's advantage. His reputation as a barrister was formidable.

My parents took Gert out in the car and left us alone on the sunny glassed-in balcony outside the sitting-room. I sat on the divan which was Gert's bed – a sort of cuddly-toy jungle.

As soon as they had gone Mr Bernstein set up his portable tape-recorder on the table and took a quick voice test.

'I hope you don't mind this, Mrs Van der Walt. It's so much less distracting than making notes.'

'I've grown used to it lately, Mr Bernstein.'

He smiled thinly. 'The police, I assume?'

'Yes. They had a lot of questions to ask. Major Van Heerden used a tape-recorder for our conversations.'

'I have a lot of questions too. And the first is probably the most important.' He leaned forward, pale eyes intent. 'I'm pulling no punches.'

'Go ahead.'

'Are you fully and absolutely on our side?'

'How do you mean?'

'Are you prepared to do everything in your power to save your husband from a long prison sentence – *at best* . . .?'

I closed my eyes for an instant to shut out that relentless searchlight stare and the grim terrible picture of the alternative to the 'best'.

'Yes,' I said. 'I'm fully and absolutely on Kobie's side.'

'Then you must know that our only line of defence is to prove extreme provocation and extenuating circumstances. Possibly the fact that Dr Stirling struck the first blow will be taken into account, though the manager of the Krazy Kat says that your husband challenged his victim—'

'Oh, please not that word! Rob was never Kobie's *victim*—'

'Then let us say he goaded Dr Stirling by shouting, "We have to fight it out. I'm going to beat hell out of you!" The assault was undeniably intentional.'

'You can beat hell out of somebody without intending to kill him,' I retaliated hotly. 'Boxers do it all the time. Kobie's a fine boxer and the knock-out blow he struck Rob was a boxer's not a murderer's. It could have happened in the ring.'

'Quite so. Now let us go back to the events preceding this tragic climax. You realize, of course, that I've had long sessions with your husband. Also with his sister. I know the background well. Your husband has loved you since childhood. He's fought over you from his schooldays onwards. When you began to have a hearing problem he inevitably established a sort of mastery. You became more dependent on him. You retreated from social contacts and he had less and less competition to fear – till Rob Stirling appeared on the scene. Do I get the picture?'

'Clearly enough. What did Rita tell you?'

'She emphasized her brother's abiding devotion to you, his extrovert temperament, generous, passionate – and excessively jealous. She holds the theory that your husband feared Dr Stirling's attraction for you from the first moment of his association with your family, and that – in fact – he encouraged an intimate relationship between Dr Stirling and herself to safeguard his own marriage.'

'You don't miss much, do you?'

'I'm quoting your sister-in-law,' he pointed out with the grimace that passed for a smile. 'She also told me that you recently refused to accompany him to America.'

'It was because of my deafness. I found it difficult to cope in parties. I knew we'd be meeting strangers all the time – that I'd be a drag on Kobie.'

'Quite. Then Dr Stirling's friend – this brilliant ear specialist, Sherard – visited South Africa and Dr Stirling saw the opportunity of getting Sherard's opinion on your case. They persuaded you to undergo surgery. I understand from your husband that he resisted this hasty decision.'

'He wanted me to wait – to have the operation later in Johannesburg. As if I'd pass up the chance of a world authority performing such a delicate operation on me!'

'Mrs Van der Walt, do you know that your eyes are flashing and your cheeks are flushed at the recollection of that trans-Atlantic telephone call when, I gather, your husband and Dr Stirling had an argument?'

'Rob was very upset; and I was resentful. Furious! It seemed to me that Kobie simply hadn't bothered to . . . to . . . project himself into my problem. It's a very distressing problem – particularly for a young woman, Mr Bernstein.'

'I appreciate that. And no doubt you felt that Dr Stirling was deeply sympathetic.'

'He really cared. He encouraged me to go ahead in spite of Kobie's objections. The result was a . . . a sort of miracle. I could hear again – join in things without making a fool of myself. My confidence came back. I felt young again. Attractive—'

This time his disenchanted smile actually reached his eyes. 'As indeed you are, if I may say so. And one result of all this was that you were drawn more closely to Rob Stirling. And he to you?'

I shrugged and looked down at my hands. I was fiddling nervously with the round ears of Gert's beloved teddy bear. Mr Bernstein cleared his throat.

'In fact, Mrs Van der Walt, you had an affair with him.'

When I remained silent, he wiped his spectacles thoughtfully before continuing.

'On his return from the States you were cool towards your husband—'

'I'm going to have his child.'

'I'm coming to that. He had reason to believe that this child was not his and that you intended to leave him for Dr Stirling – to go to Australia with him.'

'That's not so. None of it.'

'Your husband believed it was. When he . . . assaulted Dr

Stirling, your husband was under the impression that not only was he losing his wife to her lover, but also his young son. You had left Mr Van der Walt and taken Gert into hiding. With great persistence he eventually found you – with Dr Stirling at the Krazy Kat – "oblivious of your surroundings and anybody else" is how he put it to me. Are you surprised that he was provoked into aggressive action?'

I didn't look at Mr Bernstein. I noticed that the bear was missing an eye.

'One more question, Mrs Van der Walt. May I have your complete attention?'

'You have it.' I saw that his face had grown stern.

'Very well then. Why did you pick up that bottle and strike a savage blow at your husband's head – felling him, as he stood? Did you wish to do him grievous bodily harm?'

'No, *no*! I hoped to stop the fight. To stop Kobie harming Rob any further.'

'He could have harmed Rob Stirling no further.'

'I didn't know that at the time.'

'Well, then, I put it to you that you struck your husband that blow because you saw the intent to kill in his face. It wasn't the fight you wanted to stop. It was *murder*.'

I flung up my head and faced him defiantly: 'I've given you my answer. I have nothing to add to it.'

His acid smile was satisfied. 'Well done, Mrs Van der Walt.'

The trial of the State v. Jakobus Gerrit van der Walt was heard in the Cape Town Supreme Court in mid-November.

I was seven months gone and Dr Rabinowitz wished to spare me the strain of being present.

'My husband is charged with murder,' I said. 'I am the chief witness for the defence. I must be there.'

He'd considered my pale stubborn face and given in.

'Very well, but I insist you have a trained nurse in attendance throughout.'

'Daddy will be with me. Mummy will stay at home with Gert. I'll be all right.'

'I insist,' he repeated.

So Sister Worsley, who had already arranged to see me through the first month of the new infant's life, saw me through those harrowing days in court too.

Somehow, in spite of Dr Rabinowitz's warning, when the time came, I was unprepared for the full emotional strain.

It was only when we went up the steps of the Supreme Court through a jostling crowd of curious spectators that I had my first real inkling of the ordeal ahead. Many of the faces turned towards me were actively unfriendly, and although I was flanked by my father and Sister Worsley, I felt vulnerable, a heavy clumsy target for righteous condemnation.

Inside the building it was cool and dim after the blinding sunshine of the city streets, and already the court-room was packed, a bare but impressive theatre with an eager inquisitive audience avid for the drama of a young man – already much in the news for the new hope he had brought a stricken area – on trial for killing his wife's lover. Even the child I carried was suspect. I had expected the clinical impersonal atmosphere of justice. Instead, I knew myself to be the object of hostility – one of the leads in a cruel real-life entertainment. Along one wall the Press bench was jammed with reporters.

A uniformed official showed us into a pew beside the empty dock. Daddy had observed that Ma and Rita were already seated, so he pushed Sister ahead of me. Rita kept her face averted. After her fashion, she had loved Rob with all she had to give, and, in her eyes, it was I who had indirectly destroyed him. My mother-in-law turned briefly towards Daddy and me, her grave eyes holding recognition of the strain on all of us. Mr Denny and Advocate Bernstein looked round from their table laden with law books, and greeted us with a nod of encouragement. In their legal gowns they were impressive. Mr Bernstein had briefed me well.

Then I saw Ma stiffen and heard the expectant stir of those who had queued for hours to see the young man who was now brought into the dock.

Kobie! The shock and heartbreak of that moment almost made me faint. Daddy's hand, strong and cool, covered mine and my unborn infant shifted as a swarm of butterflies set my tummy trembling.

Kobie had steadfastly refused to meet me – 'not till after the sentence', he had told Mr Bernstein – so it was here, in the dock, that I saw my husband again for the first time since that night at the lake. All the years of our lives – his, Rita's and mine – good, bad, happy and sad, ran through my mind as he stood to attention like a soldier while the judge, in scarlet robes, marched on to the dais, followed by the two assessors.

How could it all have led to this? A boy with frank eyes and curly fair hair, with courage and a quick temper – the 'golden lad' my grandmother had admired, the bridegroom my parents had approved for their daughter, the devoted father of my children – ending up *here*, pleading Not Guilty to the crime of murder.

His strong profile was expressionless and proud – my Kobie, whose every mood was always reflected in his face like a breeze passing over grainlands. He looked very young and alone, his face pale and drawn, his shoulders braced as he refuted a charge totally at variance with his true nature. Once he turned to look at his mother and sister and me, his expression wounded and puzzled, as if he too was at a loss to know how all this had come about.

I don't remember the trial in any detail. Most of the evidence was factual and not conflicting, though much of it shocked me. Naked truth – unadorned by reasons why and excuses for – was ugly and frightening. Once I found myself staring at the judge, longing to shout, 'But you don't understand *why*! I can explain!' His was not a smooth academic face. It was rugged and direct, as if he too had known strong human passions. 'He's an odd customer,' Mr Bernstein had told us. 'His justice can be rough, but it's usually fair. We may be lucky.' The assessors, two experienced legal men, looked dry and enigmatic to me.

They referred to Kobie and Rob as 'the accused' and 'the deceased'. It sounded inhuman.

Those who had witnessed the fight at the Krazy Kat told the story succinctly. Daddy gave evidence that Kobie had admitted to taking benzedrine tablets on his long drive south, had refused food at the flat, but had asked for brandy. Yes, his son-in-law had appeared 'distraught' when told that his wife was with Dr Stirling at the Krazy Kat.

Mr Bernstein put Rita into the witness box to help build up his case of extreme provocation. She swore that the deceased, her lover, had been estranged from her by her brother's wife, thus contributing to the disturbed state of the accused's mind. But it soon became apparent from the prosecuting counsel's cross-examination that he meant to turn 'extreme provocation' into a double-edged weapon and establish it as the motive for a murderous premeditated attack.

When I went into the witness box I was aware of the hush in court. Sister Worsley stood near me; I was allowed to give my evidence sitting down, and Mr Bernstein guided me skilfully into the effects of my hearing problem on our marriage and on my emotional attitude towards 'the deceased'. Once or twice I glanced up at Kobie's sad troubled face and choked over my answers. The judge, who had many questions, asked them gently. The prosecuting counsel never let up. He had beetling brows and prominent teeth.

'Mrs Van der Walt, why did you pick up that bottle and strike your husband with all your might?'

'It was the only way to stop the fight.'

'Did you think that unless you could knock him unconscious your husband would kill Dr Stirling?'

'I knew he would hurt Dr Stirling.'

'Fatally?'

'My husband is a very good boxer and very strong. He is a fighter, but not a killer.'

'Not even under extreme provocation?'

Mr Bernstein was on his feet protesting. At last I heard the words:

'No more questions.'

Then Kobie took the stand, a grim, gaunt young man, despising prevarication.

The prosecuting counsel, black-browed and aggressive, showed him none of the consideration he had shown me.

'Did you intend to kill the deceased when you went to the Krazy Kat in search of your wife – "distraught", as one witness has described your state of mind?'

'I intended to beat hell out of him, as you've already heard. I saw him with my wife, and I saw red.'

I couldn't endure watching Kobie standing there at bay, his life and his freedom at stake, goaded by dangerous questions flying at him like poisoned darts.

'I put it to you that you were maddened because you believed your wife was planning to leave you for the deceased and was moreover with child by him.'

Suddenly the potted air in the soundproof court stifled me and everything about me blurred and whirled. I don't know if or what Kobie answered. All I heard was my own voice, shrill and agonized, crying out in an attentive silence.

'I never meant to leave you, Kobie! And this child is yours! You *must* know that!'

I was vaguely aware of a hubbub, of the rapping of the judge's gavel and of Sister Worsley calling urgently for an ambulance to be summoned.

My father and Ma were leaning anxiously over me as the first contraction seized my body.

24

THE HOSPITAL

A FEW HOURS LATER, WHEN THE THIN SICKLE MOON of Ramadan was rising in the eastern sky, I heard the first feeble cry.

'Nearly two months' premature – but perfectly formed.' Dr Rabinowitz gave a huge sigh of relief which I echoed.

Mummy, who had been with me at Groote Schuur throughout the later stages of my labour, said, 'Look, Jo! Your daughter . . .'

The sister held the doll-like baby, wrapped in a blanket, for me to see. Tiny chiselled features, pointed chin, surprisingly thick dark hair, and long delicate fingers. I turned away. I'd fought these many weeks to save a son – fair like his father. The little dark doll was taken away and placed in an incubator in the intensive care baby ward.

Dr Rabinowitz was holding my pulse.

'She's extremely exhausted,' he said to my mother. 'The strain of the last few days – and now this. She must rest.'

I found myself back in the same room where not so very long ago – or was it a hundred years ago? – we'd battled to avert this infant miscarrying. I was tidied up and wearing the nightie Mummy'd brought for me with my little make-

248

up case. I couldn't bother with make-up, but Mummy brushed my matted hair. Within minutes I fell asleep.

I dreamt that Kobie leaned over me and whispered, 'She's a beautiful baby, liefie – just like you.'

When Liz came to see me next morning I was awake and refreshed.

Her clear eyes smiled at me.

'I've seen your daughter. Congratulations, Jo!'

'Can anything so tiny survive?'

'Of course. Just give them a chance to get her established. She's showing her mother's tenacity as it is.'

I told Liz about my dream. She's always keen to know about dreams. But her smile only widened.

'After your outburst yesterday afternoon, the court was adjourned. Your husband and his mother came straight here to the hospital. He only went back to his hotel in time to bath and shave before putting in his appearance this morning for the summing-up.'

'You mean Kobie – and Ma – were here when my baby was born?'

'Very much so.'

'Then they've seen her?'

'Of course. Mrs Van der Walt says her grand-daughter has Kobie's ears—'

'Faun's ears – oh, Liz! Are you telling me it *wasn't* a dream – Kobie leaning over me—'

'It wasn't a dream. He was here but he wouldn't wake you. You were pretty dopey.'

'Mummy?'

'She's gone back to the flat – to Gert. She'll bring him here later today. Your father's in court.'

'When will we know . . . the verdict?'

'It's expected some time this afternoon. Perhaps sooner.'

'Then Kobie'll come to me afterwards?'

She hesitated.

'If he's able to . . .'

The room, full of summer sunshine, grew suddenly cold. It blurred for a moment and came back into focus. My hands were clammy and my mouth was dry. It was difficult to speak.

'Could I have another blanket? It's turned icy.'

'Of course. Try to keep calm, Jo. Your father's promised to ring me from the court immediately there's any news. Meanwhile Sister'll be along quite soon to take you to the incubator-room.'

The noon gun on Signal Hill boomed and I glanced at my watch. I'd forgotten to wind it. I set the hands to twelve o'clock and wondered once again what was happening in the crowded Supreme Court. All morning I'd been suffering from a sort of breathless indigestion, a need to sigh or yawn to relieve intangible pressures in the region of my heart.

I'd seen my baby and marvelled that anything so frail could have a grip on life at all. Her ears? I hadn't noticed them when first the sister had held her up for my inspection. Now I saw that they were indeed highly individual. Neat, close-fitting with familiar intricate convolutions – like Kobie's in miniature, like Gert's.

When would Kobie see her again? Would the law give us a chance to rebuild our shattered marriage? Could faith once broken ever be restored?

I was sitting in the armchair with a rug over my knees. The wardmaid came in with a lunch tray.

'No, nothing, please. I couldn't – not now.'

'Some soup,' she suggested.

'Just a cup of tea. Nothing else. Weak, with lemon.'

She fetched the tea and set it beside me. The lunch trolley rattled on its way along the corridor.

I leaned back and closed my eyes. Anxiety pressed in upon me. Surely by now there should be a message from the court! Through the open window I could hear the river of traffic surge round Hospital Bend. Less than a year ago that sound had been part of a miracle. There'd been footsteps I'd never heard before but had instantly recognized. Rob, who'd never walk these corridors again or stride along the beach or scramble up the mountain tracks. Rob, who'd launched the miracle that had proved a boomerang. If only Liz would come and shoo away these haunting memories, if only she'd bring news of what was happening. Her step, light, but not quick like a nurse's, always gave me a lift. My ears were strained to catch every sound. Suddenly I was sitting up, tense, my hands gripping the arms of the chair.

A long stride, firm and purposeful, was coming towards my room. I tried to read its message. He opened the door, disregarding the *No Visitors* sign, and the next moment he was lifting me bodily into his arms. He sat down and cradled me against him.

'Jo, my little love . . . Liefie, I'm free.'

The weak helpless tears poured down my cheeks. His jacket was open and his thin summer shirt was soaked with them.

'The verdict?' I stammered.

'Assault. Common assault with extenuating circumstances – extreme provocation. The judge found no evidence of intent to commit murder. The fact that the blow caused a cerebral haemorrhage was accidental. The sentence was lenient – a fine and six months—'

'Prison!'

'Suspended for three years on condition nothing of the sort happens again.'

'Thank God.'

But what now? The Press had made a Roman holiday of this case. Our private lives had been thrown to the lions. Even our premature infant fighting for survival had been spattered with the mud and blood of a scandal that would die hard in our small community. From a loved and trusted figure in his own territory, Kobie would now be known as a man capable of unrestrained violence, and I, his wife, as a faithless woman.

'Jo, there's something I have to know. When you hit me with the winebottle – a damn near lethal crack – *why* did you do it?'

'All that was asked and answered in court.'

'Half answered. You said you wanted to stop me harming Rob. But it goes round and round in my mind that perhaps you ... just simply wanted to kill *me*. You hated me—'

'I didn't hate you! I never have. I was terrified – for you even more than Rob. I saw murder in your face, Kobie! I had to save you from yourself, somehow. There was no other way. You were past listening or caring.'

'So you're telling me it was *me* – not only Rob – you wanted to save?'

'It was you. Rob as well, of course. But if ever a man saw red it was you that night. You were beyond thought – driven by plain primitive impulse. I'm not a violent person, Kobie, but I acted by instinct too—'

'Too late, my Jo. So all my life I have to live with that – the knowledge that I killed a man – a decent man – because he'd fallen in love with my wife—'

'That wasn't why you attacked him the way you did.'

I lifted my tear-streaked face to look straight at him, and saw the desolation in his eyes, the hollows under his cheekbones. I touched the crisp fair hair at the back of his head and felt the long scar. Even his habitual tan couldn't hide his pallor.

'You attacked him because you thought I loved Rob, that I meant to leave you, that this baby was Rob's.'

Our gaze was locked. We had reached our moment of truth.

'Yes,' he said slowly. 'You're right. Thinking that – brooding on it when you left me, taking Gert with you – turned me into a madman when I found you together, there at the lake, dancing, looking at each other as only people in love can look.'

He paused and I waited, knowing what must follow. He said:

'Was I right – in what I thought – in any part of it?'

'I never meant to leave you, and this baby is yours. If I believed myself in love with Rob, it was a mixture of attraction and the deepest gratitude. Something that wouldn't have lasted. He wasn't for me any more than he was for Rita. He belonged to all those who needed him.'

'You needed him?'

'For a while – yes. He was sorry for me. He wanted to see me enjoy life again like any normal girl. If I hadn't been deaf in the first place, none of this would have happened—'

'Wouldn't it?'

'No, Kobie. When Rob came back into our lives at Springbok Spruit that spring, I'd already changed – begun to retreat. You know that. You tried to bring me back – to keep me in the swim – but it took a miracle—'

'Yes,' he said slowly. 'When you wouldn't come with me to America I felt as if I'd lost you. You were going your own way . . . into yourself . . .'

So he too had recognized the U-turn – that 'lonely road' his mother had recognized – away from the world of people, back into self.

He held me for a while in silence. I rested like a child on his lap, vaguely conscious of my own recovered thinness and of his familiar strength and robust quality, strangely sublimated by the suffering and stresses of the past weeks. I

waited for the question he was surely bound to ask – the
when and where and how, and then the scene, the old cycle
of mistrust and aggression.

But when he spoke again I knew that now he would never
ask those questions about Rob and me. He said:

'Between us all, we destroyed him – a force for good.'

'Yes. You, me – Rita too. And fate.'

I raised my head from the crook of his shoulder and gazed
at him. His face was grave, his sunken eyes dark blue in the
shadowed sockets. My man of the sunlit plain had passed
through dark barren regions since last we had been together.

'You tried to save me from my part in Rob's destruction.
It was too late, and you failed. Is it too late for us to save
our marriage, liefie? Can we do it – together?'

I touched his cheeks, the hard, fresh skin I knew so well,
the hollows that were foreign to him. Could we go back
to Springbok Spruit and remake our lives without recriminations?

'Are you sure you want me back – after all this?'

'More than anything in the world. We need you – all of
us at Springbok Spruit. Gert, this tiny new baby, Ma – even
Christabel and Annie—'

For the first time a vestige of a smile touched his eyes –
light in the darkness.

Springbok Spruit. Nothing wrong had ever happened
there. Our home had seen no disloyalty at any time. It was
only here, in the shadow of the granite mountain I had
feared from adolescent schoolgirl days, that danger had
entered and disrupted our lives, bringing much that was

good and wonderful and more that was bad and dreadful in its wake.

My fingers found the scar on Kobie's bowed head as I drew his face down to mine.

'Kobie, my darling. I want to go home.'